It was too quiet

Bolan hurried up the gravel driveway to where the tour bus was parked. Along the far side, he found the bodies of the American tourists he had been sent to protect. A scatter of empty brass lay in a wide arc in the dirt. Shining Path had pumped hundreds of rounds into them at close range. Those not killed outright by automatic fire had been finished off with contact head shots. The side of the bus was dimpled with bullet holes and splattered with blood and bits of bone.

Just below the line of the passenger windows, one of the mercenaries had left orange spray-painted graffiti: The Lord of the Seas.

Don Jorge Luis Samosa had thrown down the gauntlet.

MACK BOLAN ®

The Executioner

DON PENDLETON'S
THE EXECUTIONER®
DAYHUNT

Lord of the Seas
Trilogy

Book II

A GOLD EAGLE BOOK FROM
WORLDWIDE.®

TORONTO • NEW YORK • LONDON
AMSTERDAM • PARIS • SYDNEY • HAMBURG
STOCKHOLM • ATHENS • TOKYO • MILAN
MADRID • WARSAW • BUDAPEST • AUCKLAND

First edition July 2000
ISBN 0-373-64260-1

DAYHUNT

Printed in U.S.A.

Justice is always violent to the party offending, for every man is innocent in his own eyes.

—Daniel Defoe

I will never admire my adversary. His actions are selfish, and usually at the expense of innocent lives. He has earned my judgment, not my respect.

—Mack Bolan

THE
MACK BOLAN®
LEGEND

Nothing less than a war could have fashioned the destiny of the man called Mack Bolan. Bolan earned the Executioner title in the jungle hell of Vietnam.

But this soldier also wore another name—Sergeant Mercy. He was so tagged because of the compassion he showed to wounded comrades-in-arms and Vietnamese civilians.

Mack Bolan's second tour of duty ended prematurely when he was given emergency leave to return home and bury his family, victims of the Mob. Then he declared a one-man war against the Mafia.

He confronted the Families head-on from coast to coast, and soon a hope of victory began to appear. But Bolan had broken society's every rule. That same society started gunning for this elusive warrior—to no avail.

So Bolan was offered amnesty to work within the system against terrorism. This time, as an employee of Uncle Sam, Bolan became Colonel John Phoenix. With a command center at Stony Man Farm in Virginia, he and his new allies—Able Team and Phoenix Force—waged relentless war on a new adversary: the KGB.

But when his one true love, April Rose, died at the hands of the Soviet terror machine, Bolan severed all ties with Establishment authority.

Now, after a lengthy lone-wolf struggle and much soul-searching, the Executioner has agreed to enter an "arm's-length" alliance with his government once more, reserving the right to pursue personal missions in his Everlasting War.

PROLOGUE

Sea of Cortez, 1:35 a.m.

At the helm of the twenty-eight-foot open boat, Martinez Miguel Martinez plowed through the stiflingly humid night without instrument or navigation lights. Warm air rushed over the Lexan windshield, buffeting his face. Ahead, bathed in starlight, the sea gleamed a greasy black; the bow of the Super Panga rose and fell as it sliced through widely spaced swells. Martinez could feel the throb of the twin Yamaha 250-horsepower outboards through the soles of his bare feet. From the deck vibration and the pitch of the engines' whine, he estimated his speed at sixty-five miles an hour.

The Super Panga, Martinez's pride and joy, had been custom built in La Paz. The *Estrella Fugaz* wasn't designed for any of the usual Baja pursuits—sportfishing, waterskiing or skin diving. It was a specialized work vessel, meant to carry small, heavy cargos long distances at high speeds in the dead of night. Lashed under nonreflective, plasticized tarps on the fore and aft decks were ten fifty-kilogram bales, the property of the Samosa drug cartel. Entrusted to Martinez's care, a thousand pounds of high-quality South American marijuana was heading north.

To his left, about three miles away, desert mountains

formed an impenetrable black silhouette. Above their jagged peaks the sky was choked with stars. The glittering points of light jolted and spun wildly as the bow split the southerly swells. The stars' erratic movement was disorienting, making Martinez dizzy. Squinting against the warm wind, he maintained a constant distance from the Baja peninsula, steering toward the barely visible landmass that lay before him, the low, uninhabited island known as Isla Monserrate.

Martinez Miguel Martinez had come to drug smuggling relatively late in life. He had worked as a taxi driver, had commercially fished for squid, had been a field hand at a produce farm and had helped build rich gringos' condos. Every job he'd ever held had been temporary and had paid him miserably.

Until this one.

He had earned enough money in his first smuggling run to pay for the fully outfitted *Estrella*. Twenty-nine thousand dollars, cash.

As he neared Isla Monserrate, the swell diminished, the rise and fall of the bow ceased. It was like driving over black glass. He opened the lid of a small container sitting on the console and took a plastic fork from his T-shirt pocket. He held the container under his chin and used the fork to shovel its contents into his mouth. Cold cactus salad was part of the supply of food his wife had packed for the journey. Despined, peeled, cooked strips of cactus leaves tasted like string beans, and his wife had tossed in raw onion, sweet red pepper, a touch of garlic, lemon juice and diced serrano chile. Also on the console, in another sealed container, were thick, handmade corn tortillas. Beside it was a dented steel thermos of strong, black, heavily sugared coffee.

Martinez financially supported not only his wife of

five years, but several girlfriends as well. He also provided for four infant daughters, two by his wife in Cabo
San Lucas, one by his girlfriend in La Paz and one by
his girlfriend in Loreto. He bore these responsibilities
with a light heart and a sense of humor. That he had laid
claim to so many pretty young women and produced so
many babies gave him much status among his male
friends. Though he never bragged about it, most people
knew that he worked for Don Jorge Luis Samosa, the
renowned Lord of the Seas. He wasn't shunned because
of this. After all, the Samosa organization was the big-
gest corporation, in terms of gross profit, the Mexican
equivalent of Microsoft. And smuggling was a time-
honored, much-romanticized profession on the Baja.

Once a month for the past two years, he had made the
difficult, dangerous, thirteen-hundred-mile run from
Cabo San Lucas to San Felipe, at the northern end of
the Sea of Cortez. The one-way trip took four days,
sometimes more, depending on the weather. Martinez
traveled mostly at night, especially in and around the
larger towns, where the Federal Judicial Police based
their helicopter patrols. When the sky started to lighten,
he would find a rocky cove and anchor there, pulling
camouflage netting over the boat. He slept under the
tented netting, on top of the marijuana bales, until sunset,
then moved on. A four-wheel-drive pickup truck would
be waiting for the cargo on the beach at San Felipe. The
return trip always took longer because Martinez stopped
on the way to see his girlfriends and play with his children.

Over the steady scream of the engines, Martinez
thought he heard something. A distant, beating sound.
He immediately cut back on the dual throttles.

It was there, all right.

A steady *whup whup whup whup* coming from the darkness to his left, near the mainland.

Against the dead-black cliffs, he saw a moving light and recognized it as a helicopter's marker beacon. The aircraft was heading in the same direction he was, but holding tight to the coastline. With the plastic fork still clenched in his teeth, Martinez tossed the salad container onto the console.

There was only one helicopter in service in the Loreto area.

And it belonged to the Federal Judicial Police.

He spit out the fork and pounded down the throttles with his fist. The *Estrella* rocketed forward, its engines redlined, propellers spewing a towering rooster tail of foam. In a heartbeat, he was doing seventy-five miles an hour, racing for the cover of the far side of Monserrate.

Two days earlier, under the same circumstances, he wouldn't have bothered to alter his course or speed. He had never had problems with the police because he always followed the rules: run at night, and skirt the narrow surveillance overflight zones.

Now there were no rules.

This thanks to the arrests of the corrupt, high-ranking Mexican military and government officials in charge of stopping the drug traffic. Without a steady downward trickle of cartel bribes, there was no protection for the likes of Martinez Martinez. Local authorities who wanted to prove they weren't tainted, and thereby avoid jail themselves, were coming down hard on any smugglers they could catch. Rumor had it that the Federal Judicial Police were now authorized to destroy suspected drug boats on the spot. Because of the vastness of the Baja and the puny scope of the government air patrols, Martinez knew the odds were still in his favor, assuming no one had tipped off the authorities that he was making a smuggling run.

When Martinez reached the southern tip of Isla Monserrate, he throttled the motor back to a crawl. He listened intently as the sound of rotors faded towards Loreto. Relieved, he powered up again.

As he cleared the end of the four-mile-long plateau of upthrust volcanic rock, the Super Panga began to pound into the swells that had stacked up along the windward side. Martinez ran so close to the shoreline that he was engulfed by the ammonia and rotten stench of fresh guano. Monserrate had healthy populations of pelicans, gulls, snakes, scorpions and flies.

He beat his way to the north end of the island, where a hook of eroded cliff shielded a shallow lagoon from the wind and waves. In the starlight, he could see the waves breaking over the bay's narrow entrance. He had timed his arrival to coincide with the peak of the high tide. The water was deep enough for him to enter, if he was careful. He waited for a big swell, then eased the *Estrella*'s throttle, and was lifted over the barrier and into the placid bay. Immediately, he hit the power-tilt switch, tipping his motors part way up to protect their props.

He then risked a flash of console-mounted spotlight to pinpoint the wind-sculpted pinnacle that marked the middle of the lagoon. From it he located the path through the reef structure to the strip of beach that was his destination. With the floodlight turned off, he edged the Super Panga forward. Twenty feet from the shore, he shut off the motors and power-tilted their lower units completely out of the water.

After running the bow of the boat onto the shore, he replaced his Miami Dolphins cap with a Petzl headlamp, which he switched on. He quickly stepped into a pair of shin-high rubber boots, a defense against snakes and scorpions. Hopping down to the ground, he dragged a bow line across the brick-colored dirt to a pile of rocks and made it secure.

The air was dead still and suffocatingly hot. He climbed the rubble of the collapsed bluff to a shallow opening, a wind-cut depression thirty feet above the waterline. The cave was just deep enough to hold a dozen, five-gallon cans of gasoline. His cousin, a commercial hand-line fisherman from Puerto Escondido, ten miles to the north, kept the cans full in return for monthly cash payments. The Monserrate cache was one of a series of fuel stockpiles hidden along the desert coast that made the trip possible. Each cache was maintained by a different relative or trusted friend.

Two at a time, Martinez lugged the cans down to the shore, then swung them into the *Estrella*'s bow. As he hoisted the last one over the rail, in the distance he heard the beating noise again. Faint. The helicopter had turned 180-degrees and was very slowly backtracking its route along the mainland coast. He immediately shut off his headlamp.

The *federales* were clearly looking for somebody.

Martinez's best option was to leave Monserrate at once, to head north at top speed. Unfortunately, the Super Panga's gas tank was almost empty. He carried just enough fuel on board to reach the next cache, which allowed him to trim weight and maximize speed. Without a partial refueling, he wouldn't get more than a few miles before running out of gas.

Two by two, he quickly hauled the gas cans to the stern. Kneeling on the deck, he unscrewed the fuel tank access cap. Normally, he used a plastic siphon hose to transfer the gas from portable containers to the main tank, which minimized spillage. Under the circumstances, it was too slow. He dropped a funnel into the access port, twisted a spout on one of the cans and tipped it toward the hole.

Though refueling went much faster, pouring gas into a funnel was a messy proposition, even in broad daylight. In his haste, Martinez sloshed a good deal of it on the deck and on his clothes. The spilled fuel ran back into the bilge pump as well. That didn't concern him much. He figured he could hose down the deck and his pants with seawater once he was safely underway. As he emptied the last can, the noise of the police helicopter peaked, then began to grow fainter as the aircraft continued to fly south.

Maybe he was letting himself get spooked over nothing. There were any number of reasons why the government aircraft might have turned back toward La Paz.

Martinez hauled the cans back to the bow. He considered throwing them out on the beach and shoving off. But the urgency of the situation had faded. If someone other than his cousin found the containers and reported them to the police, he would lose Monserrate as a refueling site. Anyone with half a brain could guess what the cans were being used for.

After turning on his headlamp, Martinez lugged the cans, six at a time, back to the cave. He picked up a football-size white quartz rock that sat beside the entrance and carried it to the foot of the cliff, a sign to his cousin that the cans needed refilling.

As he untied the *Estrella*'s bowline, he heard the *whup-whup-whup* sound again. Only it was louder and more crisply defined. The helicopter had once again reversed directions. It was heading north, and its line of flight had changed.

The *federales* were running a grid search of the area. Someone had turned him in.

Frantically, Martinez pushed the bow off the beach and pulled himself into the boat. He lowered the engines to their shallow-running position and hit the ignition key. As he reversed, pivoting for the bay's entrance, his hopes sank. From the noise building behind him, he could tell that the helicopter had reached the southern tip of the island and was rapidly closing on his position.

He slammed the dual throttles forward. The sudden burst of acceleration made him grab for the wheel to keep his balance. With a sickening lurch, the Super Panga blasted through the waves breaking over the bay entrance, blasted through it and angled up. For an instant, the bow pointed skyward, engines screaming as props churned nothing but air. The *Estrella* crashed down and shot forward, colliding with, then flying over the tops of the onrushing swells. Martinez fought to maintain control of the helm.

Eighty miles an hour was fast, but the police helicopter could do better than 120.

Over his shoulder, Martinez saw its beacon appear above the island's bluff. Its searchlight flashed as it dropped to an altitude of fifty feet. The blinding glare of the floodlight swept past the stern of the *Estrella,* then swung back and locked on.

They had him.

Martinez glanced at the .308-caliber Heckler & Koch G-3 assault rifle racked on the console's side rail. He knew if he could hit the helicopter's tail rotor, he could bring the aircraft down. But if he opened fire, the *federales* would certainly shoot back with their own automatic rifles, spraying the Super Panga's deck, trying to hit him, the engines or the gas tanks. Martinez wasn't a good enough shot to take the risk.

"Stop! Shut off your engine immediately!" a voice hailed through a loudspeaker, as the helicopter pulled directly in front.

Martinez responded by suddenly veering left, out of the circle of the searchlight. Stopping wasn't an option. Stopping meant arrest and the confiscation, if not immediate destruction, of the boat. Without the Samosa bribery network, Martinez would rot in jail. Without the *Estrella Fugaz,* his loved ones would go hungry and be thrown out of their houses.

The helicopter followed him.

Martinez swerved away from the blinding glare and stinging rotor wind. As he did, he caught a glimpse of the aircraft's side and its open bay door. Automatic weapon fire crackled down at him and a volley of bullets whistled across his bow.

He didn't slow. He hoped the *federales* wouldn't shoot to kill, as long as he didn't fire back. With a full tank of gas, the Super Panga had much more range than the helicopter. If he could evade it long enough, the pilot would have to turn back for the airfield or crash into the sea.

The helicopter swung around to parallel his course. Another burst of autofire sailed over the bow. Through the helicopter's loudspeaker, a voice roared, "This is your last warning. Stop now!"

Instead, Martinez turned away, cutting a mad zigzag. The helicopter followed, swooping directly over him, its spotlight illuminating the deck, its rotors' wash whipping off the tarps that covered the marijuana bales. Martinez caught sight of something small and dark dropping from above. It hit the bales and bounced forward onto the bow. As he ducked, instinctively, the helicopter swung away.

A thunderclap and flash of fire simultaneously shook and lighted up the *Estrella*'s bow. Flying shrapnel shattered the windshield of the center console. The grenade's concussion hurled Martinez away from the helm. He hit the deck hard, on one knee. Miraculously, he was unhurt by the explosion. The cargo had absorbed most of the shrapnel and the blast hadn't ignited the gasoline on the rear deck.

With no one steering, the Super Panga spun wildly to the right.

Martinez grabbed for the wheel and continued the turn, heading back for the island. It wasn't a rational decision, but he didn't know what else to do.

The helicopter swung around behind. Its searchlight beam raced up his wake.

Unable to outrun the pursuer, Martinez tried another, last-second change of course. The helicopter hung overhead for an instant before he cut the wheel. Long enough for someone inside to throw another grenade.

The fragmentation bomb landed on the bales. It didn't bounce this time, as the marijuana cushioned the impact. Over his shoulder, Martinez watched the grenade roll off the bale, onto the deck, then down into the bilge well.

Out of reach.

Martinez had no choice. He jerked back on the throttles and threw himself over the port-side rail. As he cleared it, the blast from behind lifted and spun him. He cartwheeled through a ball of flames into the warm, black sea.

He regained consciousness underwater, choked as he tried to breathe, then kicked for the surface. Coughing and gasping for air, he dog-paddled. Already forty yards away, the *Estrella Fugaz* was dead in the water and burning like a torch. Dense clouds of smoke rolled from the marijuana.

The police helicopter tightly circled the wreckage, flying low, pinning it with the searchlight. Martinez saw bright flashes coming from the open bay door. They were taking photographs—to document the kill.

As he tread water, Martinez noticed a sharp, steady pain in his lower back. He assumed he'd wrenched it when he'd hit the water.

After only a couple of minutes, the helicopter wheeled and headed back for Loreto, leaving him bobbing in the rapidly dwindling firelight. The *federales* hadn't even bothered to look for him, alive or dead.

Martinez turned toward the darkness and Monserrate. He had the waves behind him and he was a strong swimmer. It was only a half mile to the island. He set off with determination and confidence. After a few dozen strokes, an awful weakness came over him and he had to stop.

Something was wrong.

It was all he could do to keep his head above water.

He realized then that he had been wounded by the grenade. His blood was pouring out into the warm sea. His arms and legs felt impossibly heavy, his head was spinning. He let himself relax and floated on his back, rising and falling with the waves. A great sadness filled him. A sadness that he would never see his children again.

1

Yucatán, Mexico, 9:40 a.m.

Sweat dripped off the end of Harlan Klein's wide nose. Slumped in the shade outside a Mayan stone temple, absolutely hammered by the tropical heat, he mopped his face with a cotton hand towel he had draped around his thick neck. Klein wore a white, sleeveless T-shirt emblazoned with the words *Gold's Gym*. A place he had never been.

From somewhere inside the ruins, which sloped into the top of the hillside, the Mexican tour guide's voice echoed unintelligibly as he prattled on in high-pitched, pidgin English. Klein had refused to step over the tall threshold and follow the rest of the group into the relative coolness of the temple. Constructed of tightly fitted stone blocks, the thousand-year-old building was divided into a series of small, interconnected rooms with high steepled ceilings. The dirt floor reeked of centuries of accumulated bird and bat shit.

If he wouldn't set foot in a derelict building in the States, except at gunpoint, why the fuck would he do it when he was on vacation?

All Klein wanted was to get back to the four-star hotel in Cancún, to the pool, the bar and the air-conditioned ocean-view suite. He never would have left it if his current girlfriend and traveling companion, Tanya, hadn't insisted that they do something besides eat, swim, drink margaritas by the pitcher and have sex.

Something to improve their minds were her exact words.

Which, it turned out, meant climbing impossibly steep flights of slippery stone steps without handrails, in the blistering heat.

Klein put up with Tanya's ditzy ideas because she was hot, fifteen years his junior, leggy, slim and blond. Even though her hair color obviously came from a bottle, it drew enthusiastic comments from every group of young Mexican men they had passed since their arrival three days earlier. As Klein could do nothing about the whistles, kissing sounds and catcalls, except make a complete fool of himself, he pretended they weren't happening. Or that he didn't understand precisely who they were directed at.

Still talking a blue streak, the tour guide returned to the temple's entrance and led his flock back outside. The flow of exiting bodies forced Klein to stand and step into the sunshine. It made him wince. As a child he had amused himself by torturing ants with a magnifying glass. He wondered if this was what the ant felt in the instant before it burst into flame. His T-shirt and shorts were soaked through, as were his socks. His toes squished inside his Air Jordans. The gold Rolex on his wrist and the gold chain around his neck felt like they weighed ten pounds apiece. Tanya, in cutoff jean shorts and a pink tube top, her blue eyes wide with mental stimulation, stepped to his side while the tour guide continued his rapid-fire narration.

The little Mexican had a number of nervous ticks, which irritated Klein. If he wasn't clearing his throat or jingling the coins in his pockets, he was suddenly thrusting his arms out in front of him to shake his watch and ID bracelet down his wrists. Equally annoying to Klein was the tape loop of subject matter the guide relied on. A very short tape loop.

Stepping to the edge of the temple walkway, with a sweep of his arm the guide directed their attention to the low tree-covered hills that surrounded their position. "They may look like natural mounds of dirt," he said, "but they are not. Under each of them is another buried temple, waiting to give up its ancient secrets."

Whoop-de-do, Klein thought. If the Mayans were such brainiac supermen, where the hell were they now?

While the guide explained the extensive road network, Klein surveyed his fellow American tourists. With the exception of Tanya and himself, they were an amazing collection of knock-kneed underweight geeks. Most of them were seniors wearing matching broad-brimmed canvas sun hats with securely tied chin straps. Their white, hairless, spider legs were set off by black socks and sandals. Who else would willingly leave a four-star poolside and the endless thong parade for piles of un-composted bat shit and fallen-down stone huts? Not only were these nerds entranced by the guide's endless repetition of facts, but to add insult to injury, even those twice Klein's age weren't sweating as much as he was.

"I hope you have all enjoyed your visit to Xiche," the guide said. "The next site on our tour will demonstrate a different sort of architecture. I think you'll find it very fascinating." With that, he started down the long flight of steps.

While the others hurried after their guide, Klein hung back, mopping himself with the towel. The stairs led to the temple's ceremonial plaza and, below that, to a broad parking lot and the waiting bus. Klein checked his watch. He had another six hours of this torture to endure. Tanya had insisted on the full-day tour.

She hooked her arm in his as they descended the stone steps. "I'm so glad we decided to do this," she said merrily.

Klein's thoughts were as dark and nasty as temple mold. Even though Tanya had a great body, was good in bed, a decent cook and she had her own money, thereby fulfilling all of his basic requirements for a female companion, this mind-improvement crap of hers was a considerable off-putting and offsetting downside. If he couldn't break her of the habit, she would have to go the way of the Mayans.

By the time they reached the bus, the sweat dripped off the hem of his T-shirt and shorts and ran in steady trickles down his bare legs. As he climbed the steps into the bus, a delicious wave of cold air enveloped him. The driver had the air-conditioning cranked all the way up. Klein wiped his face with the towel as he and Tanya waited for the people ahead of them to find their seats. Their driver had decorated the dashboard with a garish collection of religious icons and plastic flowers. The color photos of his family were protected by a thumb-tacked layer of cellophane. In front of the display was a white plastic bucket. The word *Tips* had been written on it in black marker. The bucket contained a scattering of soggy-looking one-dollar bills.

Klein and Tanya turned down the narrow aisle and took their seats near the rear of the bus. He immediately pointed the overhead air-conditioning nozzle at his face and opened it wide.

When all the passengers were seated, the guide picked up a microphone and began to speak to them through the bus PA system. The sound quality was awful, making him very difficult to understand.

And very easy to ignore.

Klein was doing just that, staring out the tinted window when a pair of full-size pickup trucks stormed up the site's gravel driveway and into the parking area, throwing up a cloud of pale dust. The guys who stood crouched in the beds of both trucks were dressed in camouflage fatigues and carried assault rifles. Klein had seen similar squads driving around Cancún, where they acted as security forces to protect the tourists from street crime. Unlike the soldiers he'd seen in Cancún, these guys were wearing black ski masks pulled over their faces. The trucks stopped in front of the bus, blocking its escape. Right away, the ski-masked guys jumped out with their guns.

"Shit!" Klein groaned.

"What is it?" Tanya said.

"Take off your watch and rings," he told her as he undid the clasp on his Rolex. "Do it quickly."

Klein crammed the watch, the gold necklace and his massive, diamond signet ring down into the crack of his bus seat.

"What in the world are you doing?"

"Shut up and hide your stuff or you're going to lose it," he said as he shoved his wallet down the seat crack as well. "We're about to be held up."

A commotion broke out at the front of the bus as the armed men forced the door open and pushed up the steps. Klein half stood, looking over the top of the double row of headrests. The tour guide held his ground against the intruders, shouting shrilly and shaking his fists at them. One of the robbers responded by punching him in the face. The short, quick blow to the chin sent the little guy sprawling, unconscious, into the driver's lap.

That bandit picked up the microphone from the floor. His voice came through the overhead speakers loud and clear. "Everybody out of the bus," he ordered in perfect, unaccented English. "Do this slowly and quietly and no one else will get hurt."

People began yelling and screaming at once.

The masked man pointed his weapon at the ceiling and cut loose a deafening burst of gunfire, which shut everybody up.

"I won't ask you again," he said into the microphone. "Now, get up and get out. Move!"

When Klein and Tanya's turn came, they edged past the man who seemed to be the leader. Klein got a good look at the eyes behind the ski mask's slits. Humorless, maybe even a little bored. For him, this was just another day at the office. Everything was going to be all right, Klein told himself as he descended the stairs.

The heat slammed his face as he stepped down to the parking lot. A man with an assault rifle gestured for him to move to the right. Running away was out of the question. The robbers had taken up widely spaced positions that controlled all possible escape routes. They had a definite military bearing. Like their leader, they were neither nervous nor excited. They had obviously done this kind of thing before.

Klein and Tanya joined their fellow tourists lined up against the side of the bus.

"Honey, I'm scared," she whispered up to him, squeezing his big, soft biceps.

"They're just going to rob us," he assured her. "Give them your purse when they ask for it. Don't make a fuss."

At a hand signal from their chief, the robbers closed ranks in front of the tourists, shouldered their weapons and took careful aim.

"Oh, no," Tanya moaned. "No...."

Klein surprised himself by stepping between her and the row of gun barrels.

People started to scream.

"Fire!" the bandit leader shouted.

MACK BOLAN held the speedometer needle of the Ford Taurus pinned to the post. Engine howling, the rental car rollercoasted over the low, rounded hills of the two-lane asphalt road. On both sides of the pavement was semi-tropical jungle—wall-like thickets of scrubby, stunted trees, none taller than twenty feet, none with a trunk thicker than a baseball bat.

Flying over the crest of a rise, he reacted to obstacles on the road ahead. Bolan allowed the car to drift into the empty oncoming lane to avoid a trio of men creeping up the grade on battered bicycles. Shirtless, they wore single-shot shotguns tied with rope slings over their shoulders. They blurred as he swept past.

They were professional game hunters, market hunters looking to intersect the animal trails that crossed the Yucatán highway. Once they found the paths they'd dismount and proceed on foot into the dense bush with its poisonous snakes, insects, wild boar and maybe even the odd jaguar. It was a difficult way to make a living, full of hardship and danger. And despite the risks, it offered no guarantee of success.

He understood their way of life because it was also his. More a calling than a trade, the hunt fulfilled a need as undeniable as an intake of breath. It had become Bolan's sole purpose and salvation.

A 9 mm Ingram MAC-10 lay on the Taurus's passenger seat. He had duct-taped a second 32-round magazine, bottom up, to the one protruding from the butt of the submachine gun's grip. Under his left armpit, in shoulder leather, hung a 9 mm Beretta 93-R. From the caliber, rate of fire, magazine capacity and barrel length of his weapons, a trained observer could deduce the nature of his quarry and the killzone's boundaries. The man known as the Executioner anticipated numerous, similarly armed, two-legged prey in extremely close quarters.

Seventy-two hours earlier, he had been sent to extract the young sons of Yovana Ortiz, former Mexican beauty queen and soap opera star, from a fortified rancho north of Loreto on the Sea of Cortez. Pedro and Juanito had been taken hostage by the Murillo brothers, who controlled the Baja leg of Don Jorge Luis Samosa's narcotics shipments. For years, Ortiz had acted as an intermediary for that same cartel, distributing Samosa's payoffs to high-level military and government officials. She handed out look-the-other-way money. Ramon and Roberto Murillo had kidnapped her children to keep her from giving evidence about the Mexican bribery network, evidence that could shut off the flow of cartel drugs into the U.S.

Ortiz, who was being held in a top secret location in Tijuana, had agreed to cross the border and turn over her testimony and a collection of videotaped evidence to the DEA-Justice Department joint task force based in San Diego in exchange for the return of her sons. On the flight back from Loreto with the rescued boys, the Executioner had gotten word by radio that despite all security precautions, Yovana Ortiz had been murdered while in custody, blown apart by a suicide bomber. It had fallen to Bolan to break the news to the eight-year-old Juanito and his little brother, Pedro, that their mother wouldn't be there to meet them when they landed. That they would never see her again.

Bolan's softly spoken words left poor Juanito and Pedro in shock. The boys had seen much killing and destruction during their escape. Even in the thick of it, they hadn't panicked. Whether brave beyond their years or simply numbed by the intensity of the rancho firefight, they had followed the tall man's orders and, against all odds, had come through without a scratch. Up until that terrible moment.

As the Cessna circled the Tijuana airport, Bolan had done his best to comfort them. Faces streaked with tears, the boys stared out the window, hoping against hope, despite what he had told them, to see their mother standing down there beside the runway.

Yovana Ortiz died trying to provide a new life for her children. She had put everything on the line to protect them from the corruption and violence of the drug trade. And with her last words she had given up the location of the videotaped evidence, hidden in a safety-deposit box in a San Ysidro, California, bank. Within eight hours, arrest warrants were being served in Mexico City to the top-level military officers in charge of drug traffic interdiction.

The drug lord wasn't taking the blow to his pipeline quietly. According to intel collected by Hal Brognola, director of the ultrasecret Sensitive Operations and head honcho on the anticartel campaign, Samosa had hired a team of Shining Path mercenaries to commit an act of terror against U.S. citizens on Mexican soil. Their mission was payback for the disruption of Samosa's business-as-usual, a foretaste of what would happen if the cartel wasn't left alone.

Although details of the planned atrocity were sketchy, intel had identified the target, a Caribe Line tour bus. Upon his arrival at the Mérida airport, Bolan had been met by a courier who passed to him, along with a locked pouch of weapons and ammunition, the news that while he was still in the air the Colombian slaughter squad had landed and been spirited away from the same airport by none other than Ramon "Three Nails" Murillo, the man who had orchestrated Yovana Ortiz's brutal murder for the cartel in Tijuana.

Bolan had left the airport parking lot with tires smoking. That had been three hours earlier.

Based on the schedule of tour stops Brognola had provided, he figured he was within two miles of the bus when he heard a distant, unmistakable crackle of autofire through the open window. He jammed the Taurus's gas pedal against the firewall. The engine screamed, the tachometer needle swung deep into the red, but the vehicle couldn't go any faster. His ninety-second ETA to Xiche was carved in stone.

The volleys of automatic weapon fire raged on and on. When they stopped, they were followed by an erratic string of single shots. Punctuation marks to the already completed massacre.

Ahead, on a hillside above the road, stood the pale-yellow ruins of a small Mayan temple. Next to the highway was a palapa-roofed, open-sided structure with a silver tour bus stopped beside it. In a cloud of dust, a pair of pickup trucks roared across the site's gravel parking area toward the road.

The first truck bounded onto the highway in front of him, fishtailing as it accelerated away. A half-dozen camouflage-clad men crouched low in the pickup's bed.

They held automatic rifles and ski masks covered their faces.

Shining Path.

The second pickup truck reached the end of the driveway a split second before Bolan. In that instant, he had the angle and the advantage. And he took it, aiming the corner of his bumper at the front fender of the moving truck. The other driver gawked at the oncoming Taurus in shock.

Then came the bone-jarring, metal-shrieking impact. As the G-force wrenched him sickeningly sideways, all Bolan could see was the white air bag .

The crash accordioned the right front quarter of the Taurus, spinning the car in a series of wild, counterclockwise revolutions up the road. Bolan slammed on his brakes. With wheels locked, the Taurus drifted off the far side of the road onto the shoulder and crashed to a stop against a wall of trees.

Immediately, the Executioner opened his SOG autoclip with his thumb and with a single slash of the serrated blade, gutted the airbag. Another slash freed him from his seat belt. He reached across the transmission hump, under the splintered dashboard and grabbed the MAC-10 from the floor. The windshield was opaque with spider-cracks and had buckled inward on the passenger side. Bolan shouldered open the door and bailed with the Ingram held out in front.

Over the car's roof, he saw the pickup had been knocked ninety degrees to the right by the impact and now faced him, head-on. One rifleman, who had been thrown from the truck bed, was now lying facedown in the middle of the road. Two other shooters in the pickup's bed shouldered their assault rifles, using the cab for cover.

As Bolan raced for the rear bumper, autofire pelted the Taurus, punching a line of holes along its passenger side. He didn't return fire. Instead, he crashed through the tightly woven curtain of trees. High-stepping, one arm in front of his face to protect it from the branches, he beat a path through the brush as bullets sailed around him, flicking leaves and clipping off twigs.

His goal wasn't as it appeared.

He wasn't trying to get away.

The Executioner veered hard left, paralleling the road, backtracking in the direction of the pickup. Gunfire from the highway dwindled, then stopped. Shining Path had lost him. He belly-crawled the last three yards to the edge of the jungle and peered over a low berm of dirt. His shooting angle had much improved. The full length of the truck was exposed, as were the four gunmen still standing in the bed. One of them shouted and pointed at him.

Bolan opened fire from the prone position, hosing the rear of the truck with 9 mm full-metal jackets. The shouter jerked backward as a string of slugs ripped his torso from hip to armpit. He crumpled, falling over the tailgate onto the ground. The other gunners dived from the bed to the cover of the far side of the truck.

Thanks to his low angle and the high crown of the road, Bolan could see beneath the undercarriage. He dropped his aim and pinned the trigger, skipping Parabellums into the exposed feet and ankles of the gunmen. The mercenaries fell, screaming as he continued to fire, into their now visible prostrate bodies.

The MAC-10's bolt locked back, its magazine empty. Bolan dropped the spent clip into his palm, flipped around the duct-taped spare and slapped it home. The screaming on the other side of the pickup faded, then stopped altogether. He gave the cocking handle a quick snap, then fired into the truck's tires, blowing them all out, dropping the wheels onto their rims so the opposition couldn't return fire from under the truck as he advanced.

As Bolan pushed up from the ground, the man lying in the middle of the road came suddenly to life. Assault rifle in hand, the gunner took off running down the middle of the road. After a dozen strides, perhaps realizing his back was exposed, he turned to fire.

Bolan let him get the weapon up, then he cut loose a quick burst that sent the man sprawling, crashing onto his back on the center line. Heart-shot, the terrorist barely twitched. Then he was still. Forever.

When the gunfire echoes faded, it got very quiet.

The Executioner walked over to the truck. The driver's head had been rammed through the side window by the impact. The jagged circle of glass that ringed his neck had nearly decapitated him. His blood poured down the outside of the door, spreading over the hot asphalt in a bright red pool.

One by one, Bolan checked the others for signs of life and, finding none, he pulled off their ski masks, exposing sweaty brown faces and staring brown eyes.

No Ramon Murillo.

The Executioner hurried up the gravel driveway to where the tour bus was parked, still idling. Along the far side, he found the bodies of the American tourists he had been sent to protect heaped on the ground. Some still had camera straps looped around their necks. A scatter of empty brass lay in a wide arc in the dirt. Shining Path had pumped hundreds of rounds into them at close range. Those not killed outright by automatic fire had been finished off with contact head shots. The side of the bus was dimpled with bullet holes and splattered with blood and bits of bone.

Just below the line of the passenger windows, one of the mercenaries had left orange spray-painted graffiti: *El Rey del Mar*. The Lord of the Seas.

Don Jorge Luis Samosa had thrown down the gauntlet.

2

Military Garrison Number One Headquarters, Mexico City, 2:35 p.m.

One by one, Hal Brognola placed the color faxes on the interview room table in front of General Augusto Patan. In wrist and ankle shackles and a gray prison jumpsuit, the Mexican army officer studied the collection of grainy, overly contrasted images. The hard glare of the caged ceiling light and the pictures' poor quality underscored the savagery they captured. In them, blood and shadow were the same, an indistinguishable shade of black.

After a moment, Patan looked up from the snapshot horror. Beneath wildly sprouting black eyebrows, his dark eyes glittered. "So, the snake bit you," he said. "You stepped on his tail. What do you expect?"

Brognola stared into the man's scar-pitted brown face. The "snake" he referred to was Don Jorge Luis Samosa. General Patan had sold himself to the international drug lord, surrendered without firing a shot in the one and only campaign of his military career.

"This is no longer just about drugs," Brognola said. "The mass murder of American citizens in Yucatán was a terrorist act. There will be a heavy price to pay."

The prisoner's gaze remained steady and cool as he answered, "So what?"

"Unless you cooperate with me, you'll be the one to pay it," Brognola assured him.

"That's absurd! I wasn't involved in the killings, but even if I was, this is not the United States. You have no authority to prosecute me here."

Brognola paused, then said, "I suppose you think, after things settle down in three or four months, your life in prison will be pretty soft. You'll be able to pay to have anything you want brought inside the walls—color TV, leather couch, Persian rugs, your mistresses. You think, sooner or later, when all the right people have been paid off, you'll even be able to walk out of here a free man."

Patan didn't try to hide a smile.

The big Fed took a thick file folder from his open briefcase and carefully set it on the desk in front of him. He laid his hand on it, palm down. Beneath his spread fingers the embossed Department of State emblem was visible. Looking the man straight in the eyes, he said, "Your case has been expedited by the highest levels of the Mexican and the United States governments. It seems you're a great source of embarrassment to your own people. One they would like to bury. General Patan, you're about to be extradited to the United States on federal charges of conspiracy and aggravated murder."

"You can't prove that I had anything to do with the murders of those tourists!"

Brognola leaned over the table and spoke in a voice barely above a whisper. "Hey, I don't have to prove a thing, because you're not going to make it across the border alive. You're not even going to make it out of Mexico City."

Patan leaned back in his chair. He measured Brognola and his threat. "You're bluffing," he said. "And it's a bad bluff, at that. The U.S. Justice Department would never condone my assassination, or anybody else's."

"Like you said a minute ago," Brognola said, "we're not in the United States."

"More empty bluff," Patan countered. "Your credentials say you work for Justice. Are those credentials false?"

"The question is irrelevant. Whoever I work for, this stack of official documents demands that Mexican military authorities surrender you to my immediate custody. And no matter how much bribe money you've got squirreled away, it isn't going to do you any good. I can't be bought off."

Patan glared at him.

"Your partners in crime are coming along for the ride, too," Brognola said. "When Colonel Anibal Montego and Major Jesus Gomez-Herrera see what happens to you, they'll fall all over themselves to cooperate." The big Fed slid the file folder across the table. "I trust you have your affairs in order...."

As Patan leafed through the sheaf of legal papers, his face fell, his arrogance suddenly gone. Self-assurance gone. What seemed impossible was in fact a done deal. According to the papers before him, he was already the property of the United States government.

"After I call for the guard," Brognola told him, "you and I will proceed out of this prison and go directly to my vehicle. Make any kind of fuss and I'll have you sedated and dragged out by your heels."

Patan stared down at the manacles on his wrists, his jaw muscles clenched.

Brognola could read the miserable coward's mind. He

was thinking, in Mexico anything could be made to happen. All it took was power.

Something the general was fresh out of.

When Patan finally looked up, words signifying yet another surrender tumbled from his mouth. "What sort of cooperation do you want?"

"As I said before, I need the location of Don Jorge Luis Samosa and an accurate physical description of him."

The general was incredulous. "But I can't give you either," he protested. "I was telling you the truth when I said I don't know where he is, and that I've never met him face-to-face. My dealings were only through the dead woman, Yovana Ortiz."

Brognola had heard the same story many times before. No verifiable photos existed of the self-proclaimed "Lord of the Seas," the criminal who boasted absolute control over maritime drug smuggling to North America. All the eyewitness descriptions that had been collected to date were either contradictory or otherwise suspect.

"Then give me the name of someone who does know," Brognola said.

"The Murillo brothers, Ramon and Roberto. They have a history with Samosa. Back to the beginning."

Brognola shook his head. "That's no good. The Murillos have both disappeared."

"I know where they are," Patan insisted. "I know exactly where you can find them."

"I'm listening."

"Roberto Murillo was badly injured by grenade shrapnel during the battle at his Baja rancho, but he survived his wounds. The evening of the attack, he fled Mexico in a private plane. His destination was San José, Costa Rica."

"And how do you know this?"

"The plane's copilot telephoned me shortly after they landed and the ambulance took Roberto away. He knew I would pay him well for such information. The copilot said Roberto will be in the plastic surgery clinic of Dr. Hector Perpuly for several days at least, while his face is operated on and he recuperates."

"And his brother, Ramon?"

"I know nothing about his escape from Tijuana, or the attack on American civilians in the Yucatán. I assume he'll join Roberto in San José. The Samosa cartel has much influence there."

Brognola retrieved the file folder, dropped it in his briefcase, snapped the lid closed and rose from the table.

"Is that all?" Patan asked.

The big Fed pounded once on the room's steel door with his fist. A uniformed guard waiting outside opened it immediately.

"Are you done with me?" the general repeated.

"Not by a long shot," Brognola said. He stepped into the hall and the guard clanged the door shut. The big Fed followed his escort down the grim, windowless corridor.

The documents stacked in his briefcase were forgeries. Though they were good ones, they would never have withstood real scrutiny. He'd had no official authorization to remove the man from prison, let alone assassinate him.

A bluff was only as strong as the bluffer.

And as far as officialdom was concerned, the interview with Patan had never taken place.

They passed through a steel gate that blocked the hallway. Another similar barrier lay ahead. Because this was a military prison, everything was spotless; because it was a Mexican military prison, everything was well-worn, the center of the linoleum floor dulled from foot traffic and scrubbing with hand brushes. Brognola knew that as long as General Augusto Patan had access to his offshore bank accounts, he would never get down on hands and knees beside his fellow inmates and labor over that shabby stretch of tile. Brognola had, of course, already assigned some very skilled people to the job of finding those accounts. Once located, they could be frozen, even confiscated. In the general's near future, the spectre of the scrub brush loomed large.

The drive back to the U.S. embassy gave Brognola plenty of time to think about the big picture.

Two years earlier, the President of the United States had made the private decision to wipe the Samosa cartel off the face of the earth. This was in response to the flow of drugs undermining American society, and in response to the criminal organization's exploding financial power. Power that was starting to corrupt federal law enforcement, just as it had done south of the border.

A rogue state without borders.

The operation against the Samosa cartel was three-pronged: two public and one ultrasecret. Eighteen months earlier, at the President's insistence, congress had authorized funds to upgrade the Mexican navy so it could dominate the sea routes used by drug smugglers. This included the construction of high-speed drug-interdiction vessels (DIV); ships capable of sophisticated satellite surveillance, and equipped with state-of-the-art weaponry. Built in Mexico, the ships were to be manned by that nation's military with the help of a limited number of American technical advisors. Once launched, this new DIV fleet would squeeze off the flow of Samosa's drugs like bicoastal tourniquets.

Thanks to Yovana Ortiz, the second element of the campaign, the dismantling of the cross-border bribery network that allowed drugs to move past land and sea checkpoints, was now underway. A vital element of the overall plan, it ensured that once the DIVs were on patrol they would have maximum impact on smuggling traffic.

The President had realized that the launching of the fleet and the destruction of the bribery network didn't guarantee the end of the cartel. With the billions of dollars Samosa had at his disposal, replacements for the jailed officials would soon be found, the newly imposed sea barriers to the drug trade would be compromised and the floodgates reopened.

The only sure way to kill the beast was to cut off its head.

Accordingly, the assassination of Don Jorge Luis Samosa had been at the top of the President's off-the-books agenda from day one. He correctly reasoned that Samosa's sudden removal from power would leave his international syndicate in chaos and bring on a series of turf battles between would-be successors, who could be much more easily and efficiently dealt with.

When linked together, the three parts of the Samosa operation became a combination of punches, body blows leading to a knockout. Until this morning, the public elements had been advancing right on schedule.

The massacre in the Yucatán changed the priorities. The President had anticipated the clear and present danger brought forth by the drug cartel's economic power. Samosa intended to finance an army of professional terrorists to wage guerrilla war against the United States. The new threat had to be answered, and quickly, even though all the elements for the planned clean sweep of the cartel were not yet in place. Brognola had agreed with the President's assessment, that given the current situation, the only viable option was Samosa's immediate termination.

It took a little more than twenty minutes for Brognola's car to cover the two miles between the military prison and the U.S. embassy compound. In a secure room in the complex, he arranged for an immediate, scrambled telephone call.

Mérida, Yucatán, 3:15 p.m.

THE DESK CLERK put down the phone and exited the cramped office. Outside, in the middle of the hotel's courtyard, stood a magnificent tree. Its massive trunk and spreading branches filtered and blocked the tropical sun, plunging most of the atrium in deep, relatively cool shade.

At the base of the tree, a man sat behind a small marble-topped table, beside a fountain. Shafts of sunlight dappled the tile floor and gleamed off his dark hair, still wet, slicked back from a swim in the hotel pool. He had a half-empty bottle of beer in front of him and he was writing something in a little book. Icy blue eyes looked up from the page.

To be watched by those eyes gave the little clerk a strange and uncomfortable sensation. This hotel guest could have been a professional athlete, a soldier or the bodyguard of some millionaire. More than simple physical power, he radiated an intense quiet and total self-containment. His level of detachment was unusual, but at the same time familiar. Jarringly familiar.

"Señor," the clerk said timidly, "there is a telephone

call for you. You may take it in the office. Please follow me."

The man whose documents said he was an American named Mike Belasko picked up his little book, pushed back his chair and got up.

Standing, he was even more impressive.

So daunting, in fact, that the clerk took an involuntary, full step in retreat. Like the *balaam*, he thought. In the ancient Mayan language, *balaam* was the word for jaguar.

Like many of his contemporaries, he lived in a world of superstition mingled with incomprehensible science, a world in which the mythology of a glorious lost past was constantly reflected off the meager present. Mayan culture held that, from time to time, special men appeared out of nowhere, as if materialized from the air by the gods themselves. These beings had the power to reshape the world, to crack it in their hands like a giant hen's egg, spilling forth torrents of human blood.

With an awful, absolute certainty the clerk knew that the one who loomed over him was just such a man. On weak legs, he led Mr. Belasko to the hotel office and pointed out the phone. After the tall man entered the room, the clerk stepped outside and pulled the door gently closed. Shutting his eyes tight, he crossed himself several times.

3

San José, Costa Rica, 5:35 p.m.

At the sounds of shrill screaming, Roberto Murillo opened his eyes. Above him he could see the cloudless Baja sky. Beneath his back and legs were the hard ruts of the sunbaked road. His whole body throbbed from its shrapnel wounds. Each time it pulsed, his ruined face felt like it was about to explode.

From his right there came a frantic rustling. Though it hurt for him to move, Murillo twisted his head around.

The buzzards had landed.

When he'd last seen them, they'd been mere specks overhead. Now, dozens of them jostled, black wings flapping, talons dancing on the backs of the corpses of the gringo expatriates who had been part of his rancho crew. Facedown in the dirty sand, Ryan and Edwards had already lost their eyes. Having stolen the gringos' ears as well, the vultures rooted under the bloodied cheeks for prized tidbits of soft tissue. Competing carrion birds jerked out clumps of the dead men's hair and scalps with their beaks. Another of the expatriates, Fat Carlson, sat, eyeless, his skull stripped down to the glistening red bone.

Not all the birds were caught up in the feeding melee. Others stood calmly, just out of Murillo's reach, watching him, waiting for their chance. Waiting for him to weaken.

A shrill, bleating scream came from the other side of the road.

A human cry.

Wincing, Murillo dragged himself up onto an elbow. As he did, the buzzards scooted away, well out of his reach. In the soft dirt of the road's shoulder, he saw another fallen *compadre,* who had been crippled by the first grenade tossed out of the Cessna as it flew away with the Ortiz children. The poor bastard lay on his back, paralyzed, unable to fight off the hungry birds. All he could do was yell as they boldly walked over his legs and chest.

"God!" Murillo groaned. When he tried to push to his feet, he immediately blacked out from the pain.

He came to again as a weight settled on his left thigh. A weight accompanied by a graveyard stink. Talon points pierced his trousers and punctured the flesh beneath. Squinting up at the sun, he looked into the face of the buzzard.

Murillo was too weak to flail his arms and drive it off. The vulture took this as an invitation to climb up his body. Standing in the middle of his chest, it cocked its head to one side and stared with intense interest at his succulent right eye.

Murillo threw back his head and howled until he was breathless. The buzzard just blinked at him, riding out the storm. Then Murillo heard the crunch of boot soles on sand. Someone was approaching. He turned his head, thinking rescue was at hand.

A man in desert camo fatigues loomed over him. Tall, dark, with ice-blue eyes.

The scream "Help me!" died in Murillo's throat.

He knew this man.

The expression on his face said there would be no rescue, no mercy. Though the pale-eyed gringo stood almost directly over the buzzard, the bird didn't scurry away from his long shadow. Nor did it proceed with the attack. The vulture seemed poised, as if awaiting a command.

For the first time since he'd been a small child, growing up abandoned, an orphan in Tijuana's worst slums, *El Azote,* "the Whip," knew soul-shattering fear.

The vulture gripped the muscles of his upper chest with its talons, and with wings outspread, it slashed its beak down at his unprotected face.

Murillo jolted wide awake, gasping for air.

For an instant everything around him was a blur. He didn't realize that his left eye was covered with thick bandages, as was the side of his face. More bandages constricted his chest and his right knee. His mouth tasted of clotted blood.

Focusing with effort, he took in the unfamiliar surroundings: the white tile ceiling, the pale-green walls, gauzy curtains over the window, stainless-steel bed rails. Steady electronic beeping sounds came from the wall behind and above him. Roberto Murillo struggled weakly against the padded wrist restraints that held his hands against the bed frame.

"Ah! He is finally conscious," someone said.

A man in a starched white coat leaned over Murillo. Short and stocky, his brown-skinned head was bald. Murillo recognized Dr. Hector Perpuly, and events of the previous days came back to him in a torrent. More than an hour after the gunfight at the foot of Bahía Concepción had ended, the Loreto police had summoned their courage and returned to the scene. They had found him still alive among the strewed bodies, and raced him back to Loreto. The little hospital there wasn't equipped to repair the damage to his face or leg. The paramedics had stopped the bleeding and gave him enough morphine for the plane ride to Costa Rica.

Dr. Perpuly whipped out a penlight and shone it in Murillo's face, checking the reaction of his right pupil. "You're coming along nicely, Roberto," he said as he adjusted the flow of painkiller from the drip bag hanging beside the bed. He turned to someone and said, "Don't make him talk too long. He will tire quickly." With that, the doctor left the recovery room.

"You're a hard bastard to kill," Ramon Murillo said.

Roberto moaned and sank into the pillow.

"Don't go back to sleep on me," Ramon warned him. "We have to talk."

"Okay," Roberto said, licking his dry lips.

"We got some shit going on, Brother. Everything is messed up. I got rid of Yovana for Don Jorge, but before she died she gave her evidence to the Feds. The little bitch named names. All our top military friends have been arrested and, to get off with lighter sentences, they're giving up anyone else who ever took a bribe. There's no more protection for our shipments. The fucking judicial police are burning the goods and killing our drivers. Everything we struggled for is swimming in the toilet and is about to be flushed."

Roberto's half brother was working himself into a fury. An unpleasant thing to witness. When riled, the man nicknamed "Three Nails" was capable of explosive, insensate violence.

"And to top it all off," Ramon went on, "you managed to lose Samosa's kids."

"There was no way I could stop that," Roberto insisted. "I did everything I could."

"That's what I told Don Jorge. I said you couldn't help it, you almost got killed trying to protect them and if you'd pressed any harder Pedro and Juanito might have died. At least they're still alive, and we could get them back."

Roberto knew how difficult it must have been for Ramon to admit defeat to Samosa. Like trying to swallow broken glass. The Murillo brothers had a reputation to protect, earned over many years in Tijuana's mean streets. They dished out the ass-kickings—they never took them. "What'd he say to that?"

Ramon shook his head. "Don Jorge is crazy mad about the damage to his business and losing his boys. While you were still in surgery this morning, I was in the Yucatán, helping some Colombian terrorists kill a bunch of gringo tourists. We slaughtered them like fat pigs. On Don Jorge's orders. He has declared war against the United States. We've got to be real careful from now on. There can't be any more fuckups."

Ramon let this sink in for a moment, then said, "He knows you're badly hurt. At some point soon, though, he's going to want to talk to you about what happened at the rancho, about what went wrong. To keep us both safe, brother, I need to know the truth before he does. Who hit you? How did they get the kids?"

Roberto shut his right eye. Though their styles—and fathers—differed, the Murillos were Mexicans, obsessed with machismo. Roberto thought of himself as a commander, more detached, less volatile, less hands-on brutal than his brother. He didn't want to admit his failure, to expose the staggering ineffectiveness of his defensive plan. But he had no choice. If they were to survive the wrath of the drug lord, Ramon had to know everything.

"The attack came in the middle of the day, shortly after you flew to Tijuana," he said. "It penetrated our outer perimeter defenses without raising an alarm. When our first warning came, it was already too late, the hacienda was under assault."

"How many of the enemy did our men kill?" Ramon asked.

Roberto was silent.

"Could you identify who sent them from their gear or clothing?" Ramon prodded.

Roberto steeled himself, then said, "We killed none. We wounded none. We took no captives. Of all the men we had defending the rancho, I was the only one to survive."

"So the bastards attacked with superior numbers," Ramon said. "I figured as much. Was it a combined air and sea assault?"

Roberto felt his face flush. This was the hardest part to admit, the most shameful evidence of his failure. "I saw only one man," he said. "A tall, dark-haired gringo."

"One? There had to have been more than that!"

"There was only one. He killed most of the soldiers inside the rancho, then took out the boys I had sent overland in one of the pickup trucks to block him at the main highway. Ramon, I did everything right, and it all still went wrong. Before pursuing the gringo, I even sent a man cross-country on an ATV to get into sniping position and keep the truck from reaching the highway. In case that didn't work I had set up a roadblock with the Loreto police, but they backed out when they saw the firefight at the end of Bahia Concepción. Even then we might have recovered the boys, but a small plane appeared out of nowhere and dropped hand grenades on us. The Cessna landed on the road and picked up the man and the children. By that time everyone but me was down. When I opened fire on the plane, it circled back and hit me with another grenade.''

Ramon stood, silently fuming.

Roberto couldn't tell if his brother believed him or not. To his own ears, the story sounded wild and impossible. "This guy was one step ahead of us all the way," he went on. "He countered everything we threw at him. He turned the rancho into a pile of rubble. On his way out, he blew up the aviation fuel and the drugs we had stored in the hangar.''

"Who the fuck was he?''

"I have no idea. All I know is, we couldn't stop him.''

"What about the plane that flew him out?''

"It was a single-engine Cessna. I didn't get the serial numbers.''

"They were probably false, anyway," Ramon said. "Your lone gunman had to have been working for the Feds. His mission was to get the boys back so Yovana would give up her evidence. Strange that they would send one man and not a whole SEAL team. The Feds don't usually work that way. They like overwhelming odds. Rather use too many than too few.''

"Unless they didn't want the job tracked," Roberto suggested. "This guy left nothing but bodies and bullet holes.''

As Ramon considered everything that had been said, Roberto's eyelids started to feel very heavy. He had to fight to stay awake.

"Our immediate problem is Don Jorge," Ramon said. "We can't tell him the story you just told me—not if

we want to live. We have to come up with another one,
a better one, something he won't question. You're the
only survivor of what happened, and other than your
word, there's no way for Samosa to know how many
men attacked the rancho. We can say you got hit by an
overwhelming military force. Special Ops, black heli-
copters. You fought hard but you were outmanned and
outgunned.''

Without uttering another word, he slipped into
unconsciousness.

THE EXECUTIONER sat in a parked car up the street from
the plastic surgery clinic. His vehicle was a taxicab.
Upon arriving at the San José airport, he'd paid a cabbie
a wad of cash for the ten-year-old beat-up four-door. The
maroon Toyota was indistinguishable from the
thousands of other taxis on the streets. Bolan slumped
low in the driver's seat, watching the sunset fade. The
neighborhood that surrounded him was a quiet jumble
of two-story residential and commercial buildings, some
with corrugated metal roofs.

The plastic surgery clinic of Dr. Hector Perpuly had
no windows looking onto the street. Its entrance was
heavily barred; closed-circuit TV cameras scanned the
approach and the white steel gate. Admittance required
identification, in part because of the doctor's select, rich
clientele. Also because of the quantities of narcotic drugs
that were kept on the premises. San José had more than
its share of petty thugs. It was safer for them to steal
drugs from established businesses than from street
dealers.

Parked at the curb in front of the clinic's entrance was
a late-model dark-blue Mercedes with black-tinted windows. The driver had spent the past two hours detailing

the chrome with a rag, toothbrush and a shoe-shine box of various cleaning products. When, on the other side of the gate, the clinic's front doors opened and a long-faced, dark-skinned man exited, flanked by a quartet of bodyguards, the driver quickly put the detail gear back in the trunk, rolled down his shirtsleeves and slipped on his driver's cap.

Bolan recognized Ramon Murillo at once. Lean, slicked-back black hair, sharply dressed ladies' man. As brother Roberto wasn't going anywhere for awhile, Bolan was left free to concentrate on Three Nails.

When the Mercedes pulled away from the curb, the Executioner started up the Toyota and followed Murillo's car in the direction of the city center. Though it was almost 7:00 p.m., rush hour traffic still clogged the narrow downtown streets.

It was dark by the time the Mercedes pulled into a gated, guarded underground parking garage beneath the Hotel Flores, a six-story pink monstrosity that squatted over half a block.

Bolan drove past. He went several blocks farther before turning left at the Museo Nacional. After finding a parking space on a side street, he pulled on a baseball cap with the words *Islamorada, FL,* across the crown. The white T-shirt he wore had a jumping tarpon on the front. He swung the strap of a ballistic-nylon duffle style bag over his shoulder. The stickers on the sides of the bag were from various sportfishing destinations. Belize, Quepos, Rio Colorado, Key West.

When the Executioner walked through the hotel's front doors, two Costa Rican men standing in the doorway gave him the once-over, then smiled. They wore black T-shirts with the word *Security* in yellow letters across the chest. They were unarmed. One of them offered to call a bellhop to help him with his bag. Bolan declined. "No, I got it, thanks," he said, moving into the chaos of the lobby.

The Hotel Flores had its own casino, a twenty-four-hour restaurant, and a bar-nightclub. It catered almost exclusively to North American sportfishermen on vacation. There was a kind of frenzy to the place, brought on by the combination of piped-in salsa music, the flashing lights of the casino and tourists trying too hard to have a good time. The hotel, casino and bar were all owned by Don Jorge Samosa, though his name didn't appear on the deed or incorporation documents. It was one of the many legitimate fronts for his drug deals and money laundering.

Not forty feet away, the elevator doors opened, and Ramon Murillo and his entourage stepped out. Led by an animated guy, with a white-haired crew cut and dressed in a black silk shirt with a big diamond stud in his earlobe, they walked in front of the main desk and through the doorway under a neon sign that read Black Marlin Bar.

Bolan waited a few seconds, then followed Murillo through the doorway.

The bar beyond was dark and crowded. And the music was louder. As there were only a handful of tables, most of the people inside were standing. Ninety-five percent of them were American males, late-fifties and older. A row of demurely dressed Costa Rican women sat at the bar. The women were in their early twenties, mostly pretty and eager-looking.

While Bolan watched, Murillo's bodyguards cleared a path through the mob for their boss. Then they cleared a table for him as well. They didn't have to say anything to get the job done. The Americans took one look at the massive biceps and bulging necks and surrendered their chairs.

Shouldering his bag, Bolan edged up to the bar and ordered a beer.

As the bartender uncapped the bottle, the prostitutes standing on either side started nudging him.

"You want some company?" one of them shouted over the music.

"Too early," Bolan replied. "Maybe later."

She wagged her finger at him, showing off her dimples and very white teeth. "Don't wait too long, now," she said. "It's no good for your health keeping it locked up inside. It will make you sick."

The Executioner retreated with his beer to an open spot along the side wall and set his bag down beside him. Murillo seemed to be settling in. Drinks had arrived at the table and he was in a friendly discussion with the white-haired man. Bolan scanned the rest of the room.

Outside the bar's street entrance, more young women were waiting in line to get in. At the door, two security men used flashlights to check the dates on the prostitutes' government-issued health cards. All of the females in the Black Marlin were professionals. Bolan wondered how many of the middle-aged gringos had told their wives the truth, that they were going to spend their entire sportfishing vacation a hundred miles inland, shuttling hookers between the hotel bar and their rooms.

The discussion over, the man with the silver hair waved for the girls seated at the bar. One by one, they uncoiled themselves from their stools and made the exodus to Murillo's table. Three Nails was a man with a reputation for generosity. He also had an unlimited supply of cocaine.

By the time he'd finished his daiquiri, Ramon Murillo

had made his selections. He picked the three youngest, most bright-eyed of the bunch. He could have done the business in private, but from his expression, it was plain that he enjoyed demonstrating his power, both financial and sexual.

Had the Executioner chosen to, he could have taken Murillo out, then and there, with a 9 mm slug to the forehead. In the clamor of the nightclub, no one would have noticed the single shot of suppressed gunfire.

But he wasn't there to assassinate Murillo.

Bolan watched the Mexican, his bodyguards and his newly acquired female friends depart for the elevator. He let a minute or so pass, then followed them. The elevator doors were just closing as he turned for the staircase. Where the Murillo party was headed was no mystery. The top floor of the hotel had been divided into four luxury penthouses, each with a broad balcony overlooking the street.

The soldier climbed the stairs past the penthouse level and, pushing open a metal door, stepped out onto the roof. As he walked between the arrays of solar panels, he could hear the fiesta in progress on the opposite side of the building.

He stopped at the edge of the roof and unzipped the duffle bag. Its contents had been separately shipped from Stony Man Farm in a locked diplomatic pouch, courtesy of Hal Brognola. He fastened the Velcro tabs of the armored vest, then inserted its steel trauma plates. After putting on Kevlar shin and forearm guards, he shrugged into a combat harness dangling with grenades—frags, incendiaries, flash and tear gas. He checked the holstered Beretta 93-R, making sure there was a live round under the hammer and that the suppressor's barrel seal hadn't vibrated loose. That done, he put on a pair of skintight, black leather shooting gloves. The last item in the bag was a 7.62 mm SAR Galil with twin 50-round mags taped back-to-back. He'd picked the short-barreled Israeli assault rifle because it provided maximum firepower in close quarters.

Bolan stepped off the roof and dropped ten feet onto the balcony, landing lightly on the balls of his feet, the Galil ready to rip. Before him was a row of windows, all of them dark. That penthouse suite was apparently unoccupied. He poked the Galil's flash hider through a pane in the French doors, then reached in for the knob and opened it.

He slipped the assault rifle over his shoulder and unholstered the sound-suppressed Beretta. Dropping the thumb safety, he pushed into the suite. After a recon confirmed the place was empty, he moved quickly to the hallway door. Shifting the Beretta to his left hand, he unlocked the door, then opened it a crack. Kneeling, he used a very small hand mirror to peek around the corner.

The only light in the hallway came from widely spaced ornamental stanchions set in the walls. Partway down the corridor, three heavyset men stood before a closed door. They were all armed with sawed-off Remington 12-gauge autoloaders. The guards looked relaxed, but when the elevator bell chimed, the shotguns came up in a blur. As the elevator doors opened and five men exited, they immediately lowered their weapons.

The pair of well-dressed Costa Ricans and their personal security team were greeted with deference by the hallway guards. Bolan recognized them, too, from DEA surveillance video. Cartel top brass.

One of the corridor security guys knocked on the penthouse door and it swung inward. The new guests disappeared inside.

Bolan slipped the little mirror back into his harness. He nudged the door ajar and, bracing the Beretta with his left, he eased out into the hall.

4

Ramon Murillo enjoyed a good party. A party in his honor at the expense of Costa Ricans was a special treat.

He knew how much they hated him.

Behind his back they called him an animal. They hated him because he was Mexican and because he was more powerful than they were. Murillo couldn't remember a time when he hadn't been despised by someone, somewhere. As a street kid in Tijuana it was for being hungry and dirty. As a Baja crack dealer it was because he was without conscience. As a major cartel trafficker it was for his success. Long ago, public scorn had lost its sting. The contempt of other people had forged him and made him strong, made him what he was.

Behind the broad smiles and hearty handshakes that greeted him at every turn, Murillo sensed a new level of unease among his fellow cartel members. Evidently, his reputation for brutality had been much enhanced by the Yucatán business, not that he had ever found scaring the shit out of a bunch of Costa Ricans particularly challenging.

He sipped at his tumbler of straight Three Generations tequila, letting its fine-grained sensation fill his mouth.

The fear he'd seen on Roberto's face when his brother had described what the lone gringo had done at the rancho still nagged at him. Though he wouldn't admit it, that fear had pierced deep into his own heart. Ramon reacted to it the way he always reacted, with anger. He knew Roberto was no coward. Coming up, he had bloodied his hands as often and as willingly as anyone. Since then, he did what had to be done to maintain their stranglehold on the Baja drug traffic.

Yet Roberto was not Ramon. Though they had endured the same hardships as children, fought side by side in the same battles for turf, they had matured into men of different tastes and styles of violence. Ramon believed this was due to the fact that they'd had different fathers. Shortly before her own murder, when he was just seven, their mother had told Ramon about his father. He had been a copper miner, she had said, who got crazy drunk on mescal one day and had taken a machete to a neighborhood bar and hacked apart six men over some small, perhaps even imagined insult. She said that in trying to defend themselves, the victims had shot their attacker many times in the chest and face.

Ramon remained grateful to his mother for the revelation. Since that moment, when he first became aware of his birthright, he had felt pride in the blood he carried, in the nature of its machismo. Pure Mexican machismo.

Across the smoky room, a small group of the cartel's top Costa Ricans stood apart from the rest of the party guests, conferring in a huddle alongside the buffet table. They appeared to be gathering courage for a confrontation. Sure enough, after a moment, they walked over to him.

"Ramon, we have some small concerns about recent developments," Carlos Pedilla, their leader, said with a smile. "Perhaps you could help us lay them to rest?" Pedilla had thick white hair heavily pommaded straight back from a low, narrow forehead. Immense gold and diamond rings decorated his stubby brown fingers.

"I'll do my best," Murillo said. "What's troubling you?"

"We would like to know how long Don Jorge anticipates the northern shipment routes will be closed."

"Not long."

"Weeks or months?"

"Weeks."

"What about shipments coming here from the south? Will they continue to arrive at the same volume?"

"As far as I know, yes."

The Costa Rican glanced at his compatriots, then said, "You realize we can't make any money by just warehousing the product. We have operating costs of our own that we won't be able to recover. The situation puts us in a bad economic position."

Murillo nodded sympathetically. With the transport route shut down, tons of Samosa's cocaine was stuck in Central America, where the price was already low. This, while the southern producers kept making more of the stuff and expected to be paid in full for their on-time shipments. The choice was to either dump the drugs on the local market and lose more money, or sit on them and wait out the clampdown.

Murillo knew that if Samosa couldn't control his middlemen, the cartel would soon collapse under its own weight. Control meant maintaining the cash flow, keeping it trickling down from top to bottom. If Samosa allowed production to slow too much, the drug mills in South America would start looking for other high-volume buyers.

"Give it another few weeks," Murillo said. "Don Jorge will make it all work for you."

Expecting more than a vague promise, the Costa Rican spokesman frowned.

"Don Jorge isn't going anywhere," Murillo told him. "We all know he has a lot of money tied up in this country. He's practically an institution here. You don't want to make a mistake, panic unnecessarily and do something foolish that you will soon regret."

The Costa Rican gangsters visibly stiffened at his words.

"The way he brought Shining Path into the game worries a lot of us, too," Pedilla said. "Why did he have to rub America's nose in it? Why did he have to make a public challenge? It's like he's asking for trouble. And more trouble we don't need."

"Don Jorge isn't a man to roll over and play dead," Murillo said, already tired of the Costa Rican's whining. "You hurt him, he hurts you back, only a hundred times worse. That's the way he has always done business. You of all people should know that, Pedilla."

"But this is the United States government he's taking on!"

"From the beginning, it's always been us against the Americans. Where have you been Pedilla?"

The white-haired man glared at him.

"Let me explain something to you, then the subject is closed," Murillo said. "You don't have all the facts. You don't understand what our enemies have planned for us in the next twelve to eighteen months."

"So tell us."

Murillo shook his head. "You don't need to know anything. Just do what you're told."

ONE OF THE GUARDS was facing Bolan as he stepped into the hall. As the man opened his mouth to cry out, the

Beretta 93-R coughed once. A subsonic 9 mm slug thwacked into his left eye socket, snapping his head back. If the guard made a sound as he died, no one heard it over the thumping bass beat of the music coming from the penthouse.

Knees buckling out from under him, the guard slowly collapsed against the corridor wall, sliding into a sitting position on top of his dropped weapon. His two partners turned as he fell and, seeing the tall man in full body armor walking toward them with raised autopistol, tried to swung their own guns up before he could fire again.

The Executioner needed instantaneous kills. He couldn't risk a nonlethal wound or a near miss that penetrated the door or wall behind. Either would alert the cartel thugs inside the penthouse, taking away his edge of surprise. Because of this, he allowed a fraction of a second longer than usual to perfectly line up his targets before punching out two more close-range head shots.

Though relatively slow moving, the sound-suppressed 9 mm rounds still packed plenty of punch. The guards were jolted backward by skull-fracturing impacts, and hurled away from the door. Their arterial blood finesprayed in a fan shape across the wall as they, too, dropped to the carpet without raising an alarm.

Keeping out of range of the door's peephole, Bolan thumbed a pair of foam noise protectors into his ears. Then he holstered the Beretta and pulled a Thunderflash grenade from his combat harness. After priming the stunner, he reached around the frame and rapped a knuckle on the door.

The guard in the penthouse couldn't see who was standing outside. The only view he had through his peephole was of empty hallway. He clicked back the lock and opened the door a tentative inch.

"Julio?" he asked in a gruff voice.

Bolan pivoted and snap-kicked with his heel, driving the door inward a foot, slamming it into something solid: the face of the guy standing behind it. As the guard flew back, the door gave a little more. Bolan lobbed the stun grenade through the opening, put his back to the corridor wall and covered his ears with cupped hands.

On the count of two, the entire hallway rocked from the concussive blast, the wall behind him shuddered and the floor rippled underfoot. Though he wasn't looking directly at it, the grenade's bounce-back flash off the far wall stabbed into his retinas like a pair of blunt spikes. Smoke boiled through the gap in the door out into the hall. As Bolan lowered his hands, despite the muffling effect of the foam protectors, he could hear the men inside groaning and coughing.

He brought the muzzle of the Galil up to waist height, flipped the fire selector to full auto, then booted the door open wide. In a heartbeat, he evaluated the scene before him.

The grenade had detonated in the middle of the suite's crowded living room. The cartel gangsters who'd been standing closest to the explosion were lying around the smoldering scorch mark on the white rug, unconscious and bleeding from the ears, eyes and nose. Those standing a little farther away were left either blinded and staggering, or crawling on the floor, dragging their numbed legs behind them. Those in the suite's connected dining room had escaped most of the blast and flash effects and were scattering in desperation for any cover they could find. They ducked behind sofas and chairs as they grabbed for their weapons.

Bolan pinned the SAR's trigger, whipsawing the suite with automatic fire. The noise was unreal. The Galil's short barrel and NATO-caliber chambering added up to some deafening decibels, which made for maximum terror and confusion among an already startled enemy.

Submachine guns popped up over the top of the sofa and sides of the wing chairs, spraying six hundred rounds a minute of unaimed fire. The wild full-auto fusillade caught a still-blinded, stumbling drug soldier across the chest, spinning him into the rug.

Bolan's string of slugs chopped a swath through the chair and sofa backs, chewing up wood and fabric, sending stuffing and splinters flying. The traffickers crouching too high felt the eternal burn of 173-grain full-metal jackets. Unlike the subsonic 9 mm rounds he'd used in the hall, these were full-power, military loads. Skulls exploded as bullets passed through, sending a slurry of brains and bone shards splattering against the far wall and ceiling.

Seeing the devastation wrought by the SAR, pelted by its sticky wetness, those who survived the Executioner's first sweep abandoned their hiding places, scurrying for more solid cover.

Bolan tracked left, swinging a line of slugs across the heavily laden buffet table and through the running men. Caught by multiple torso hits, they twisted in midstride and crumpled to the floor as the bullet-shattered table legs gave way, sending the platters of food sliding off, crashing down on top of them.

Around the edge of the interior wall on his right, a pair of mini-Uzis unleashed more random fire. The 9 mm screamers ripped the air, clipping, then bringing down the chandelier.

Dropping to one knee, the Executioner stitched 7.62 mm figure eights into the front of the wall. Sheetrock and plaster were no defense against a hail of jacketed slugs. The submachine guns went flying as the rounds clobbered the gunmen on the other side.

Then the Galil locked back empty. Bolan dropped the spent magazine into his hand and, as he advanced, he quickly flipped it around, snapping its taped twin into the assault rifle's mag port. By the time he'd taken two steps forward, he was back in business, with fifty more live rounds to burn.

The surviving gangsters had retreated to the suite's kitchen area, where they massed fire along a shooting lane made of counters and large appliances. The blistering fall of lead forced Bolan to divert course.

The Executioner pulled a frag grenade from his harness, jerked out the pin and let the grip safety flip off. He counted to three, then rolled it through the kitchen doorway, onto the tile floor.

There was barely time to duck before the tremendous blast. It took out the sides of the doorway and sent one of the drug soldiers flying into the dining room. He slammed to the floor, skin blackened, hair smoking.

Before the mobsters could recover, Bolan was up and moving. He pushed into the ruined kitchen. One of the shooters had managed to pull himself up from the floor and was clinging to a countertop island. Half his face was covered with blood from a massive scalp wound, which splattered onto the white tile counter. He still had his Uzi in hand, though he had no strength to use it. From the expression in his eyes, shock was rapidly setting in.

Bolan shot him once through the forehead and kept moving.

Beyond the cooking area, three men were sprinting for the door leading to the balcony.

The Executioner fired a short, belt-high burst, chopping down the two closest to him from behind. As they crashed to the floor, the third man slipped out the French doors.

Bolan sprayed gunfire through the panes of beveled glass, catching the drug thug in midstride. The torrent of follow-up shots spun the man sideways over the balcony's railing and sent him for a six-story fall.

An instant before the hardman disappeared, the Galil's bolt locked back again. Bolan let the empty weapon drop to the ground and drew the Beretta. As he turned back for the interior of the penthouse, he heard the sound of bare feet running for the hallway.

RAMON MURILLO had just started to get comfortable. He'd stripped down to his silk boxer shorts. He still wore his heavy gold-link necklace and bracelet, and now sported a dusting of white powder under his nose. Sitting perched at the foot of the queen-size bed, he was giving stage directions to the trio of naked prostitutes. When the grenade detonated in the next room, he thought it was an earthquake. Framed pictures dropped from the walls, furniture shook in place and the floor rolled like a wind-whipped sea.

Then came the automatic weapon fire and the screams. And Murillo knew it was no earthquake.

At first only the one gun spoke. Instead of the shrill, canvas-ripping noise of a 9 mm, this piece let loose with the sound of rolling thunder. This was military ordnance.

And no one was shooting back.

A really bad sign.

Murillo lunged across the bed for the stainless SIG-Sauer P-229 that sat on the nightstand. As he jerked the .40-caliber from its clip holster, small arms fire erupted from the other rooms. Finally, he thought.

Then bullets started flying, zinging through the master bedroom in a spray of purely random angles and heights. They shattered the bureau's mirror and clipped chunks out of the wooden bedposts. Murillo dived onto the floor behind the bed as the prostitutes crawled toward the walk-in closet.

Who was it? Murillo thought, keeping his head down while holding the SIG ready in a two-handed grip. Who would dare?

Not armed robbers. Even the most tweaked-out meth heads wouldn't try to take on the Samosa cartel. You didn't rob somebody who, in retaliation, would hunt you down and squash you like a bug.

Not competing drug dealers, for the same reason. Besides, there was no one in Samosa's league or who would even come close. In reality, everyone dealt for the Lord of the Seas.

It couldn't have been the Costa Rican authorities, either. A country without a standing army was no match for the might of the cartel.

When the gun battle suddenly stopped, Murillo could hear the moans and groans of the wounded strewed throughout the suite. The cease-fire was very brief, a few seconds at most, then the heavy-caliber thunder resumed. As the running firefight swept through the suite, moving away from Murillo's position toward the balcony, answering fire from the penthouse's defenders grew weaker.

Whoever they were, the cartel was losing to them.

One look outside told Ramon Murillo that his best chance of survival was to flee.

As he carefully stepped over the bodies, a burst of gunfire erupted from the rear of the kitchen, making him whip around. Over the sights of the SIG, through the windows to the balcony, a muzzle-flash freeze-framed a Costa Rican bodyguard in series of ever more horrible grimaces.

Murillo dashed across the living room, jumping the bodies and the slowly burning patch of carpet in its center. He rushed through the open hallway door, then high-kicked it for the stairwell.

He didn't look back.

STANDING ACROSS the penthouse threshold, halfway into the corridor, the Executioner held the 93-R's sights on the middle of the running man's back. He drew the wide, combat trigger up to the break point. Braced against the doorjamb it was an easy shot. Ramon "Three Nails" Murillo was his for the taking. Bolan eased off the trigger and lowered his aim, allowing the half-naked man to vanish through the stairwell door.

He wanted Murillo, but it wasn't time for that, yet.

Turning back inside the penthouse, Bolan cracked the necks off several full bottles of tequila and poured the liquor over the drapes and carpet. When he tossed down a match, the fabric went up with a *whoosh* of blue flame.

On his way out of the place, the Executioner started stripping off his gear. He dumped the body armor, the combat harness and the sound-suppressed pistol. As he trotted down the corridor through the building smoke for the stairwell, he pulled the rolled baseball hat out of his back pocket and put it on.

When he reached the third-floor landing, the fire alarms went off.

By the time he stepped out into the lobby, chaos had already set in. People were yelling and pushing for the main doorway. Some were trying to escape with all their luggage and fishing gear. Bolan joined in the shoving match and spilled out onto the street with the rest of the hotel guests.

Stepping off the high curb, he craned his head back and saw the dense smoke pouring out of the penthouse. Then he heard sirens. Converging from the south and east, fire engines were coming.

Bolan continued up the street at a leisurely pace, making for the parked Toyota. He had arrived in Costa Rica with a short list of hard targets. In his mind, he put a big black *X* through the Hotel Flores.

5

San Diego, 12:18 a.m.

Special Agent Madeline De Leo jolted awake. It seemed like she had just closed her eyes, but the clock beside the bed said she'd been asleep for more than an hour. When her head stopped spinning, she sat up. Through the open bedroom door, from down the hallway, the soft sobbing that had awakened her continued. Pulling on a terry cloth robe and tying it securely, she padded barefoot out of her room and down the tile floor of the hallway. The corridor lights were on a dimmer switch turned down low. The door to the boys' bedroom stood wide open.

Agent De Leo stepped quietly inside. The arc of weak light from the hallway behind her streamed across both of the small beds. Juanito, the younger one, was crying in his sleep. His brother Pedro had his back turned and seemed to be sleeping peacefully despite the noise.

Nightmares were to be expected, given what these children had been put through. As De Leo moved to the side of Juanito's bed, the little boy began to speak. He called out for his mother in a thin, reedy voice.

De Leo grimaced. Though only an interim protector of these children, she had already formed a strong bond with them. As an expert in managing violent trauma in young victims, she knew that there was nothing she could do to soften or ease their pain. Nothing could give back what they had been robbed of. Only the passage of time could dull the intensity of their sense of loss and vulnerability. In truth, it would be years before either of them fully understood the enormity of what had happened.

In a few days Pedro and Juanito were scheduled to vanish into the Witness Protection Program. They would get new names, a new home in a distant city and new adoptive parents, most likely someone with a connection to the Bureau or the Justice Department.

De Leo had serious concerns about the emotional health of both of the boys, but particularly the older one. Pedro was still repressing all of his feelings, pretending to be a grown man, and in the process was getting wound up tighter and tighter. He needed to let it go.

Juanito started to speak again, at first making only unintelligible sounds, mewling noises. Then words spilled out. Desperate words in Spanish. As De Leo leaned over the boy's bed, their meaning sank in. Juanito was crying out for his father, begging his father to help save their mother. The boy then called out for his father by name.

With her hand poised to stroke the child's hair, to gently wake him, De Leo froze. She couldn't have heard it correctly, she told herself. It had to be a mistake.

The name the boy had used wasn't the name the Bureau dossier listed as his father. That man, a retired Mexican television actor, had been already contacted in regard to taking custody of the children and had refused. Adamantly.

In a tiny voice, the boy repeated his plea.

He called for his father, for "Don Jorge."

Agent De Leo straightened, the blood draining from her face.

Certainly it was possible.

But her immediate reaction was to try to think of a reason for Juanito's words being a mistake, or somehow that she had misinterpreted them. She wasn't privy to the dream the boy was having at that moment. She didn't know if somehow Juanito had confused things, or if perhaps was only enunciating part of his interior monologue. Missing words could make all the difference.

De Leo realized that she wanted the boy's statement to be wrong. If it were true, then the extent of these children's injury was a thousand times greater than she had even imagined.

It still might not be true, she told herself.

As De Leo backed out of the room, Juanito was still crying for help. She wanted to comfort him, but she had another duty to attend to, a duty to report what she'd just heard to her superiors.

Mexico City

AFTER HAL BROGNOLA put down the telephone, he stared at it for a long time.

Stewed across the foot of the bed and spilling onto the rug were damage-assessment photos from Costa Rica. Brognola had been in the process of reviewing them when the phone rang. Bolan had done his usual perfect job on the cartel members. The photos showed the fire-gutted penthouse suite, half-charred corpses mixed with burned furniture. Though the bodies were badly damaged, the big Fed's trained eye had picked out numerous bullet wounds. As had been planned, the Executioner had left no one alive to tell the tale, no one but Ramon "Three Nails" Murillo.

The attack wasn't a death blow to Don Jorge Samosa, by any means, but it would act as a warning shot. He would face serious problems with his top lieutenants out of the picture. That they had all been gunned down, seemingly with ease, would make those who would step into their shoes think twice. The idea Brognola wanted to get across to the cartel kingpin was that someone was playing for keeps. No rules. And that this was only the beginning.

All of that got pushed to the back of his consciousness in the wake of Agent Madeline De Leo's phone call.

If Don Jorge Samosa was indeed the father of Ortiz's children, their value to Justice had just skyrocketed. As, of course, had the nature of their tragedy.

Brognola could understand why Yovana Ortiz had kept the fact a secret. Had their parentage been made public, Pedro and Juanito would have been marked for life. Targeted not just by law enforcement, but by other drug cartels and by kidnappers. The boys would carry the mark of their father's misdeeds, and the profits he had made from them, for the rest of their lives. That she had managed to keep this from Brognola, to protect her children even as she lay dying, raised her even further in his regard. Yovana Ortiz had been a proud, brave woman.

Brognola rose from the edge of the bed and started to pace. With this new information in mind, he tried to reassemble the chronology of events. The boys had been taken by force from Tijuana by the Murillo Brothers. Brognola had believed that that kidnapping was only meant to turn them into hostages to keep their mother from talking to the Feds. He realized now that it was possible the Murillos were supposed to return them to their father.

Brognola knew very little about the man who called himself the Lord of the Seas, only a jumble of conflicting facts and suppositions. Samosa had a reputation for being incredibly violent and a generous philanthropist. He was as willing to use his billions to buy the favor of the poor as well as the rich. In some quarters in Central America he was seen as a kind of Robin Hood.

Behavioral science experts had done many profiles on him, but they invariably led nowhere. There was no way to tell fiction from fact. Except that Samosa's organization moved more illegal drugs into North America than any other single source.

It was rumored in Chiapas that he was the son of a Chiapas bean farmer; in Mazatlán that he was the son of a shrimp fisherman. It was rumored in Mexico City that he had been born into an upper middle class family and that he had attended university in Europe. None of these rumors could be verified by independent sources. Samosa had never been arrested or fingerprinted under his own name.

For the first time they might have something real to work with.

If the boy could be believed, it was something Brognola could use against Samosa. The twin tragedies of Ortiz and her sons was something he couldn't change. He had done his best to protect their mother from the Murillos.

As for the boys...

If they gave up the location of their father, Brognola knew he would use that information to terminate Don Jorge Samosa. He would make the boys orphans.

A sobering thought for any man of conscience.

The fact was, in the course of Brognola's job, people got hurt. Innocent people.

He had lied to Yovana Ortiz repeatedly about the safety of her boys in order to keep the big ball rolling. He had looked her in the eye and done it.

He would lie to her young sons, too.

6

Ramon Murillo strode down the gleaming corridor of Dr. Perpuly's clinic, bracketed front and rear by four machine pistol-carrying security men. Considering what had happened at the Hotel Flores, the extra protection seemed only prudent. Under Murillo's sunglasses, the whites of his eyes were sandblasted a bright pink from exposure to smoke and lack of sleep. He'd had a rough night. And it hadn't gotten any easier after he'd escaped the hotel.

Once he'd reached safety, he'd had a long, uncomfortable phone conversation with Don Jorge Luis Samosa. The hotel disaster had left him with a lot of explaining to do.

How was it that of all the cartel brass in the suite he alone had survived the attack?

How did the assault team manage to penetrate the hotel without raising an alarm?

Why didn't Murillo get a good look at the people responsible?

Was the massacre of Samosa's Costa Rican lieutenants payback for the slaughter of Americans in the Yucatán?

Samosa hadn't liked any of the answers. Murillo could

tell that by the dead silence on the other end of the line. The trouble was, he couldn't make sense of of it, either. The lightning strikes against the cartel had been too quick, too precise not to have been planned for months.

Planned with inside help?

And the inner fire, the animal fury that Murillo relied on, that he had used so successfully all his life was of no value to him in the situation. He couldn't respond to Samosa with anger or with threats or with actual violence. He couldn't intimidate the Lord of the Seas. He felt he was being unfairly accused of incompetence.

This was the second time in less than a week that he had been put in the position of explaining the unexplainable. First, the taking of Pedro and Juanito from the Baja rancho, which resulted in Yovana Ortiz giving evidence to the Feds, and now this.

Murillo had no doubt that the only reason he and his brother were still breathing was because of their long history with Samosa. Though there were widespread rumors about his ruthless, even psychotic temper, Samosa wasn't an irrational man. He expected and accepted a certain amount of failure in his business. But events of the past few days had begun to stink of a major betrayal, of conspiracy, of a sellout by someone. The finger of blame pointed at the Murillo brothers. They were both sole survivors of huge consecutive setbacks to the cartel's dealings. Neither Murillo brother had a satisfactory explanation for what had gone wrong.

At the end of the unpleasant phone call, Samosa had offered Murillo the opportunity to make things right, a way of redeeming himself and his brother. The offer was nonnegotiable.

Roberto was sitting in bed when Ramon entered his room, flanked by the four bodyguards. The room's wall-mounted television was turned on. While the wounded man watched the morning news, a pair of nurses were finishing changing the dressings on his injured face.

Ramon signalled impatiently for the women to leave. As the nurses scurried out, he waved for the guards to follow. They stepped out and stood silent watch in the hall.

"How are you feeling?" Ramon asked his brother as he approached the bedside.

Roberto's face looked even more swollen than it had the day before. The side that wasn't hidden under bandages had a purple sheen to it from massive bruising.

"Raw, but I'll live," came the hoarse answer.

"Your face seems worse."

"Evidently, there is some infection of the area around the surgery. Dr. Perpuly says it isn't uncommon, despite precautions. Because of the pain I couldn't sleep last night." He showed his brother the little pump device that allowed him to drip more painkillers into his intravenous line, supposedly to self-medicate as needed. He pushed the button with both thumbs, then threw the contraption aside. "Damn thing is worthless," he said. "It's set for too low a dose. I've been up watching the TV since before daybreak. What happened at the hotel?"

Ramon took a seat on the edge of Roberto's bed and retold the story of the slaughter of Samosa's lieutenants without embellishment. When he was finished, Roberto said, "Someone has targeted us."

Ramon stared stone-faced at his brother.

"Someone is trying to embarrass us in front of Don Jorge," Roberto said. "Trying to make him doubt our loyalty or to make it look like we've sold him out to the Feds or to some other cartel. Ramon, unless we get to the bottom of this and pin the blame on whoever's really behind it, we are both under death sentence.''

"What can we do?"

"We have to figure out who is after us. Think, how many men attacked the hotel? How many did you see?"

Ramon shrugged. "I only saw one gun firing."

"Then it's possible that it was all the doing of one man. The same man who hit the rancho!"

"It's possible, I suppose."

"More than possible," Roberto said, sinking back into his pillows. "We've got a tiger on our tail. The question is, who put him there? And how can we kill him?"

Ramon thought for a second, then said, "Don Jorge's found out where his kids are being kept and who has them. They're in San Diego, being guarded by FBI agents.''

"So?"

"So, there is a connection between the boys and whoever is trying to destroy us. A federal connection. Don Jorge offered me the chance to go collect his kids, and I accepted. After I get the boys, I'll make their keepers squeal like pigs.''

Ramon reached into the pocket of his slacks, fumbled around for a second, then drew something out in his balled hand. Under Roberto's nose, he opened his fingers. Laying across his palm were three six-inch-long nails.

"I'll find out who our enemy is," Ramon said, "and where they intend to strike next. We will be there waiting. There will be no repeat of what has happened before.''

"I could come along to help you...."

Ramon patted his brother on the leg. Roberto looked

terrible. Battered, exhausted, in pain. "You're still too weak," he said. "You need to rest so you can recover. By the time I return with the children you'll be better. When I come back we'll kill this tiger together. Skin it and eat its heart."

7

Mack Bolan opened his eyes at the beeping of his wristwatch's alarm. He'd slept for four hours.

Just enough.

The one-room apartment was dark. Heavy drapes were drawn over the floor-to-ceiling windows along the opposite wall. He let the alarm finish, then reached under the pillow and drew out the sound-suppressed Beretta 93-R he had hidden there. He set the handgun on the nightstand and rolled out of bed.

The Executioner shrugged into a loose-fitting, gray, short-sleeved uniform shirt. One of the pockets had a plastic-laminated identification tag clipped to it. The ID bore his color photograph and a false name. As he pulled on pants and shoes, over the gasping throb of the room's air-conditioning he could hear the roar of traffic outside the building. He cracked apart the curtains with a fingertip. Blinding tropical daylight streamed through grimy windows. Four floors down, the cars on Avenida Central were jammed bumper to bumper.

The downtown San José apartment had been prepared by persons unknown to him. Whoever they were, they had left food, drink and a laptop computer with CD-ROM. He hadn't bothered to turn off the computer before he'd gone to bed. It sat on the kitchen table, its screensaver showed brightly colored tropical fish swimming randomly back and forth. Bolan stepped to the sink, put some water in a pan, then set it on the hot plate to boil. Walking back to the table, he tapped the laptop's space bar. The fish vanished.

In their place was an architect's complex schematic, a blueprint of a large, ornate building. The three above-ground floors were connected by an elevator and enclosed staircases fore and aft. The two below-ground floors were accessible only via the elevator.

Bolan had spent three hours examining the structure of this building. It was time well spent. He had memorized every detail. Blindfolded, he could fight his way through it.

Don Jorge Samosa had purchased and converted the nineteenth-century San José mansion into a private museum eight years ago. For him, it was a perfect choice because it had two existing subground levels. And because it was of sufficient size to permanently garrison the necessary armed guards. Estimates of the Museo Paniagua's defensive force ranged from as low as thirty-five men to as many as fifty. The guards didn't go home to their families every night. They did tours of duty, twenty-four hours a day, usually ninety days at a stretch. Bolan knew the manpower estimates were probably soft. They came from a mathematical formula that used detailed observations of the amount of consumable goods trucked in and the trash trucked out.

If the Hotel Flores and the personnel in its penthouse had been important to Don Jorge Samosa's international operation, the building on the screen was its linchpin. Much of the actual wealth that Samosa held in Costa Rica was contained inside its walls. A private gold depository made things incredibly simple for the drug lord. There were no records.

How much bullion was stored on the lowest subground floor, locked behind yards of reinforced concrete
and many feet of tempered steel?

Half a billion dollars worth?

Stony Man Farm didn't know.

The DEA didn't know.

The CIA didn't know.

Bolan didn't know and what's more, he didn't care.
All that mattered to him was that it was a sizable portion
of the drug lord's net worth, the capital base for all of
his legitimate and illegitimate enterprises in Central
America.

He removed the pan from the hot plate and emptied
the boiling water into the top of a stained mesh bag
suspended in a wooden frame over a ceramic mug. The
mesh bag had been prepacked with ground coffee. It was
the Costa Rican equivalent of autodrip.

Watching the mug slowly fill, he was keenly aware of
how his tactical position had changed. He could no
longer count on the element of surprise. He had to assume that Samosa had already put two and two together
and figured out that there was a concerted, ongoing campaign to hurt him, if not bring him down. Accordingly,
the drug lord would have made every effort to defend
his most liquid assets. It was likely that the gold depository would be on high alert.

As he sipped his black coffee, Bolan reviewed everything a final time, scrolling through the entire cyberdos-
sier on the depository that Aaron Kurtzman had sent
from Stony Man Farm. When he was done, he ejected
the CD. After taking the battery out of the smoke detec-
tor on the kitchen wall, he dropped the disk into the
bottom of the pan and put it back on high heat. In a
matter of seconds the disk started to smoke, then it burst

into flame. He let it burn for a few seconds, then quenched the evil-smelling fire under the faucet.

There was nothing on the computer's hard drive to connect it with him or with Stony Man Farm or with the United States government, so he didn't bother destroying it. He figured that the laptop would disappear without a trace, anyway, long before any local law enforcement agencies came knocking. All he had to do was leave it behind. The free computer would more than make up for the stink and the ruined pot.

Bolan unscrewed the Beretta's sound suppressor so the weapon fit easily into his waistband at the small of his back. He left the tail of his shirt out, covering the pistol butt. After slipping the suppressor into his pants pocket, he took a last look around the apartment, then picked up the black uniform cap hanging on a peg by the door.

As the Executioner exited the building onto the street, he put on his sunglasses. The sidewalk outside was crowded with pedestrians. The heavy concentration of cars and trucks in the street filled the air with diesel exhaust. He walked to the beat of car horns, of distant jackhammers and an occasional blast of salsa music from an open shop door. Lining the sidewalk, half blocking it and further congesting the pedestrians, were stalls and carts selling clothing, fast food, cassette tapes and fresh produce.

Bolan crossed the street at the light in a throng of other people, then continued to the middle of a block of six- and seven-story, all-concrete buildings. Street numbers were either nonexistent or erratically placed, but he knew where he was going. The soldier turned down a driveway ramp that led under one of the buildings. At the foot of the ramp was a kiosk and behind it was a linked, steel mesh barrier. The guard in the kiosk stepped out as he approached. The man wore a scarred, blue-steel .38 Smith & Wesson wheelgun holstered high on his hip.

"Hello," Bolan said, taking a claim check from his shirt pocket and handing it over.

"Hello," the parking attendant said, looking intently at the number printed on the ticket. He reached into the kiosk and activated the steel gate, which rolled sideways out of the way. Then he pointed into the garage and said, "Your car is over there."

"Thank you," the soldier told him. He passed the man a sizable wad of Costa Rican currency as a tip. Persons unknown had paid the parking fee in advance. For obvious reasons, they hadn't left the vehicle's keys behind at the kiosk. Bolan took them out of his pants pocket as he crossed the garage.

His ride this morning was painted battleship gray, with blue-tinted bulletproof slits for windows. It bore the gaudy logo of the Huerta Security Company on its steel plate doors. He stepped past the dual rear wheels around to the back of the armored car, which faced a concrete interior wall, unlocked the rear doors and climbed into the cargo compartment.

The Executioner had no plans to make off with a portion of the drug lord's gold. Even if he had, there wasn't room for it in the back of the armored car, anyway. Its cargo space had been customized to hold a considerable amount of high explosive. Overkill, in fact.

Shaped C-4 charges had been placed all along the inner edge of the roof line and the floor joins. Aside from those charges, cartons of plastic explosive sat on racks in the floor, all connected by interlacing wires and blasting caps. In the center of the compartment were two fifty-five-gallon drums. The warning signs spray painted on their sides read Highly Flammable. The drums were bracketed to the floor and suitably braced to withstand high-speed impact or collision.

Bolan made a quick check of the electronic rigging. Someone had done a great job. It was all fail-safe. There were double detonators and double power sources. No matter what happened, when triggered, the explosives were going to blow.

The armored car was nothing more than a rolling bomb.

Bolan hopped out and closed the rear doors. Rounding the side of the truck, he unlocked the driver's door. Before climbing in, he removed the Beretta from the small of his back and set it on the floorboard.

Inside, on the passenger's seat under a blanket, neatly laid out for him was a bulletproof vest with steel trauma plates and a fully loaded combat harness. Clipped to the webbing of the harness was a cigarette-pack-size black plastic box—the remote detonator. Between the driver's and passenger's seats lay two Ingram MAC-10 submachine guns. Two canvas satchels sat on the floor in front of the passenger's seat. He pulled on the vest, then shrugged into the harness and slipped the Beretta into its armpit holster.

When he turned the key in the ignition, the armored car's engine started with a powerful growl. The soldier waved at the attendant as he passed the gate. The man grinned broadly and waved back. He liked his tip.

At the top of the driveway, Bolan merged with the flow of traffic on the street, then crept south. There was no escaping the sea of cars until he got out of the city center. When he reached an industrial area a mile or so farther on, he managed to make up some of the time he had lost.

Reaching the depository, he turned left, drove another block, then pulled over to an open place at the curb and parked, leaving the engine running.

Eighty yards ahead was Bolan's target: a massive peach-colored three-story Spanish colonial building, surrounded by formidable concrete walls and extensive grounds. The entrance to the grounds was blocked by a pair of fifteen-foot-high steel gates.

He took a pair of Zeiss minibinoculars from a pouch on his harness and scanned the top floors of the mansion. A handful of armed men in pale-blue uniforms moved on the roof in front of a long, low structure. The rooftop observation post had been added by Samosa.

Bolan put away the binocs and checked his wristwatch's countdown timer.

Two minutes to spare.

His right foot resting lightly on the accelerator, he watched the little LCD numbers fall to zero.

8

The Executioner revved his engine and pulled away from the curb. He quickly took the heavy rig up through its gears, double clutching. The men defending Samosa's treasure were expecting the momentary arrival of an armored car.

But not this one.

According to the plan, Bolan was to stop at the mansion's entrance and hand over his forged documents, the Heurta identification tag and the vehicle's paperwork, which were supposed get him through the front gates without raising a fuss. But as he raced toward the closed gates, he had a gut feeling about slowing down.

A bad feeling.

Given the hit on the Hotel Flores, the guards might be under orders to call the security company and verify his bona fides before letting him onto the grounds. Facing fifty guns and a heavily fortified position, the Executioner's one chance in hell of completing the mission was to get in quick and strike hard.

Over the course of three long blocks, the armored car's speedometer needle climbed steadily to sixty, then crept up to seventy miles an hour. Because of the poor state of the road and the rattling walls of the cargo box, it felt a whole lot faster than that.

Ahead, the broad intersection was momentarily clear.

There was no stoplight guarding it, only a pair of stop signs at the cross streets. The cross traffic was waiting for him. For better or worse, Bolan had the right of way.

He bore down, pinning the accelerator to the firewall with the toe of his shoe. He was already past the bail-out point; he couldn't have stopped the heavy vehicle short of a collision even if he'd wanted to. The gate of the depository loomed in front of him.

A small delivery truck started to creep ahead of the stop sign on the right, its driver half thinking he could squirt out and beat Bolan through the intersection.

Think again.

Bolan gave a long blast of the armored car's horn, freezing the delivery truck. He swept through the intersection, still picking up speed. Already securely belted into his cross-shoulder safety harness, the Executioner braced himself for the coming impact. When he was thirty feet away, the pair of guards standing watch on the far side of the gate realized what was about to happen and dived aside to avoid being mowed down.

The armored car hit the steel barrier doing a little better than eighty miles an hour. Though buttressed and anchored in huge blocks of concrete, the gate didn't even slow the Heurta van. With a crash and a screech of shearing metal, Bolan blasted through. The left side of the gate snapped off its hinges and cartwheeled away, rolling up and over the back of one of the running guards, tearing him to shreds as it simultaneously ground him into the pavement. The right side of the gate was simply flattened by the front bumper. As Bolan roared over the twisted steel, one of the rear tires hit something sharp and blew out. The truck shimmied for a second, slewing off the long, straight driveway and drifting onto the beds of tropical flowers that bordered the lawns.

Then the ripped tire beat itself to pieces against the undercarriage and Bolan regained control of the vehicle.

The soldier aimed for the double, arched front doors of the hundred-year-old mansion. The sculptured hedges on both sides of the drive blurred as the armored car reached accelerated. He was seventy-five yards away from the building when gunfire erupted from the front edge of the roof.

Wild gunfire.

Slugs skipped off the steel plate roof of the cab and the top of the hood. A couple of them spanked into the bulletproof glass of the dark-tinted windshield, leaving small, glistening craters on the far side.

The Executioner hunkered down in the driver's seat and braced himself again as he closed on the four wide marble steps leading up to the targeted doorway. The small arms fire slowed and steadied. Methodically, bullet after bullet hammered the glass in front of him, turning it opaque, bulging it inward, but the windshield held.

Bolan licked his lips.

It was time to play crash-test dummy for real.

With a sickening lurch, the armored car hit the first step and was airborne, bouncing up and over the remaining steps and flying head-on into the closed double door. For a split second, Bolan was weightless, his backside lifted off the seat cushion, his body floating against the restraints of the safety belt harness. The sensation ended abruptly in an explosion of pain and a flash of white light that filled the inside of his skull.

White, then black.

Everything black.

The vehicle's front end acted like a five-ton steel wedge. With a deafening boom, it shattered the mansion's doors inward. The fit between the rest of the truck and entryway was less than perfect. The sides and arched top of the doorjamb clawed at the truck's overly large cargo box. Even as the masonry and timber gave way, screeching and sparking as it crumbled and shattered, it squeezed down on the body of the armored car, bringing the vehicle to a spine-snapping halt just inside the foyer.

At the impact with the front doors, Bolan was thrown forward against the safety harness, then slammed back into his seat. No amount of preparedness or anticipation, no muscle bracing, no safety belt could keep his brain from slamming into the inside of his skull. The effect was instantaneous. Unconscious, slumping sideways, he missed the shrill scream of steel scraping over stone. He also missed the sight of a terrified human figure, appearing before him the instant the doors turned to splinters, then disappearing beneath the oncoming front bumper.

The Executioner struggled to awaken from the stun sleep. Even while he was unconscious, some small still-aware part of him recognized and reacted to the danger he was in. In part it was due to the exacting discipline of his training; in part it was instinctive—the will to survive was something that couldn't be taught.

Choking on the thick dust swirling inside the cab, Bolan came to with a start. Shaking off the terrible heaviness in his limbs, he immediately unbuckled his seat belt and reached across the passenger's seat for his weapons, the matched set of MAC-10s. When he tried the driver door, it wouldn't budge. He slammed it with his shoulder and it opened partway with a loud groan. There was nothing blocking the door on the other side; it was stuck from the impact. He had wedged the armored car well into the building's foyer. It had penetrated up to its rear wheel wells.

There would be no backing out without a wrecking ball and crane.

Through the spider-shattered glass, he could just make out the parquet tile floor of the long high-ceilinged ante-room. A floor strewn with smoking wreckage, debris from the doors and the caved-in interior wall, and from what remained of a row of tall, ceramic vases that had been toppled off their pedestals. At the far end of the foyer, a double-branched marble staircase led up to the next level.

Even as the dust cloud started to settle, men in uniform appeared on the first-floor landing. Autofire rattled from above, and a flurry of bullets slapped the much-weakened armored windshield, spraying pulverized glass into Bolan's face.

WHEN CAPTAIN Lindor Suarez heard the sound of a roaring engine, he was on the roof of the Museo Paniagua, standing in the shade of the lookout post's awning. As he turned to face the depository's main gates, he could see the Heurta armored car coming up the road towards them at an extremely high speed. The armored car was right on time, scheduled to arrive every other week to drop off another small load of Samosa's bullion.

"What's that fool playing at?" he exclaimed in fury.

The men in uniform standing beside him had no answer. They simply gawked.

Captain Suarez was a man who lived for his routine. To him, it represented strength, discipline and professionalism. Chaos and unpredictability was the ultimate enemy.

A job at the Museo Paniagua was nothing to sneeze at. The pay was generous and steady. There were regular promotions and long vacations. Not to mention the three-month vacation from wives and families that the duty rotation gave them. And the food was of high quality and plentiful.

Over and above the material rewards, there was a certain esprit de corps among the guards. They had been entrusted with the protection of more gold than most people could even conceive of. They all knew who the gold belonged to, and what sort of punishment the drug cartel would mete out for dereliction of duty or theft. Along with the life-and-death responsibility came weapons training and endless defensive drills, all stage-managed by their very diligent commanding officer. Suarez knew how to keep his men on their toes, to keep them from going soft.

With a shock, Captain Suarez realized that the armored car wasn't going to stop. Speechless, he watched it plow through the front gates like they were made of tinfoil. For as long as he had been commander of the stronghold, there had never been an attempted robbery. The criminal element in Costa Rica, indeed in all of Central America, knew better than to mess with Samosa.

"Shoot! Shoot!" he yelled at the guards.

Stepping to the edge of the roof, they shouldered their Heckler & Koch G-3 assault rifles and opened fire on the speeding truck. In their excitement and eagerness, the three men switched their weapons to full-auto mode. As a result, they struggled to control their weapons' wildly climbing muzzles. Flurries of bullets veered wide of the oncoming target, kicking up puffs of dust as they ricocheted off the hood and fenders and skipped over the driveway's paving stones.

"The windows, dammit!" Suarez bellowed at them. "Quick, hit the driver!"

The shooters obeyed. Bracing themselves against the

roof's ledge, they shifted fire selector switches to semi-auto and squeezed off strings of rapid, but aimed, single shots. Suarez marked hit after hit as glass dust exploded from the outside of the windshield.

"Yes! That's it!" he cried. "Pour it on him!"

His excitement faded as he realized the effort was futile.

With a sick, helpless feeling in the pit of his stomach, Suarez watched the armored car continue to accelerate up the drive toward them. The man behind the wheel was winding the engine out in high gear, despite the rapidly narrowing distance to the front of the building.

All Suarez could think of at that moment was that it had to be a suicide attack, a suicide bomber. Trapped on the museum's roof, there was nowhere for him to run. And even if there had been some cover, he had no time to reach it.

The garrison commander was no coward. He steeled himself for whatever fate had in store. Determined at least to look Death in the eye, he leaned over the edge of the roof to follow the flight of the heavy truck as it leaped the stairs. A fraction of an instant later, it slammed into the building, three stories down. Suarez anticipated a terrible explosion and its accompanying fireball. Though there was nothing of the sort, he could feel the tremendous impact through the soles of his boots. Like the shock wave of an earthquake, it made the roof ripple and sway beneath him.

Suarez had no idea how many attackers were inside. Nor did he know how they intended to escape with their entry vehicle so hopelessly jammed into the front of the building. He didn't even know if any of the robbers had lived through the crash. All he knew for sure was that an enemy had breached the depository's ground level, and that car-bomb suicide wasn't part of their game plan.

Though the captain was taken aback by the turn of events, he was fully prepared to deal with it. For years, on a weekly basis, he had been drilling his troops in how to handle a head-on, concerted, military-style assault. They hadn't rehearsed this particular scenario, of course. He had never anticipated an armored vehicle ramming its way into the building.

It occurred to him as he pulled back from the roof's edge that there had to be another group of robbers and a second truck on the way. Another truck would certainly be needed if the attackers were going to haul away any part of the gold.

The grounds had to be sealed off.

From the men standing around him, Suarez selected two pairs of riflemen. "Take your assigned firing positions along the perimeter," he told them. "Cut off the exits. No one else gets in, no gold leaves here, none of the robbers leave, either. Use the fire escapes. Shoot straight. Move it!"

He then turned to Ernesto Rodriguez, the highest ranking officer on the roof. "You're in charge of the above-ground operation," he said. "Get the sniper teams set up on the roof, then gather the rest of the men downstairs for a flanking attack on the intruders. Don't let this mess spill outside the compound, Nesto. I want containment, total containment. Do you understand?"

His lieutenant nodded.

With that, Suarez turned toward the rooftop exit, waving for two of the assault rifle–armed guards to follow him. As he ran he unclipped the walkie-talkie from his belt and signaled the main garrison level, which was one story below the ground floor and one floor above the huge cache of drug cartel gold.

"Cebollo!" he shouted into the built-in microphone. "Goddammit, Cebollo, answer!"

When his lieutenant responded, he said, "This is not a drill. We're under attack. I'm coming down in the elevator to lead the defense."

Suarez burst through the steel door of a small, flat-topped structure, which opened on two flights of steep stairs leading down to the top floor and the entrance to the waiting elevator. As the elevator doors closed behind him and his escorts, he heard the unmistakable back-and-forth crackle of automatic gunfire coming from the building beneath him. Some of the intruders had survived the crash. A gun battle raged on the ground floor on the opposite side of the museum.

The captain's primary responsibility was to keep Samosa's gold right where it was. He had designed his defensive plan accordingly. After being notified that a robbery was underway, it was the duty of the officer in charge to immediately telephone the police. Suarez wasn't counting on their help; the call was a formality, a courtesy, part of the protocol. Given the traffic situation at this time of day, a delay in the arrival of law enforcement was a certainty. Also, if the authorities had already received reports of serious fighting at the Museo Paniagua, they weren't above arranging for even longer delays in order to avoid participating in it. The San José police were neither trained nor equipped to deal with a military-style assault.

In Suarez' opinion, they didn't have the stones for it, either.

So, it was up to him and his men to deny the robbers what they had come for.

When the elevator doors opened, Suarez faced a chest-high barricade of sandbags and the muzzles of a dozen assault rifles.

His second-in-command, Gustavio Cebollo, jumped up from behind the barrier and shouted, "Hold your fire!"

Through the elevator shaft came the sound of shooting. There was a war going on over their heads.

"I need intel," Suarez said as he stepped forward. "I need to know how many we're facing and how they are equipped. I need to know if we can take them out ourselves, if an all-out rear assault will end this. Get on the horn, Tavio. Find out what's going on."

The officer nodded, taking out his walkie-talkie. He turned away from the captain, covering his free ear with the palm of his hand to muffle the noise from above.

After a few seconds, he turned back.

Suarez could read the expression in the man's eyes. Whatever the news was, it wasn't good.

A RIFLE SLUG penetrated the battered, sagging windshield. It slammed into the back of the passenger's seat, heart high.

Staying put wasn't an option for the Executioner.

He kicked open the stuck driver's door, then leaned over the gearshift and grabbed the pair of small canvas satchels from the floor. He bailed out of the armored car, with the canvas bags and the spare MAC-10 slung over his shoulder. As he did so, the front windshield completely gave way under a hail of gunfire.

Behind the cover of the armored door, Bolan stole a peek at the opposition. Five men fired down at him, two from the landing; the rest knelt behind the marble banister of the first-floor balcony. On the ground floor, under each of the branches of the staircase was a doorway. According to the blueprints Brognola had provided, the doors both led through the middle of the building to a long, wide corridor and the elevator shaft that was his primary target. Before he could reach either door, Bolan had to cross eighty feet of killzone.

The Executioner popped out from behind the cover with the MAC-10 in his fist. Slugs rattled off the tempered steel of the driver's door behind him, sparking as they flattened and ricocheted. Firing on the dead run, he swept the landing with a withering, full-auto burst, spraying the two shooters there from left to right. Hammered chest high by 9 mm rounds, the men crumpled in slow motion, their arms flying wide, weapons dropping. One of them toppled forward over the first step, sliding down the stairs on his face as Bolan raced toward the bottom of the staircase.

The 15-round burst and its devastating effect made Bolan's surviving opposition think twice about a head-on confrontation. The men hiding behind the stone balusters ducked back out of the line of fire, giving him all the time he needed.

Reaching across his chest, he jerked the lanyard on one of the satchel charges and then unslung it, underhanding the explosive package, bowling it across the tile floor. It banked off the left-hand wall and skidded into a doorway.

Bolan veered around the foot of the staircase, out of the line of fire. With the flat of his foot, he booted open the door before him.

Counting down in his head, the Executioner long-strided for the first doorway on his right and dived through it.

As he hit the floor, the world came apart. The thunderclap of detonation was followed by a terrible, inanimate shriek and groan, and then another gut-wrenching boom. Placed in the perfect spot for maximum demolition, the plastic explosive had brought down the entire staircase. A boiling wave of debris whooshed down the hallway, through the open doorway and into the room in which the Executioner had taken cover.

Bolan pushed up off the floor. As he did, amid the churning dust, he caught movement out of the corner of his eye. He whirled. A guard on the far side of the room was also picking himself up, fumbling for the G-3 assault rifle he had dropped. Bolan stroked the MAC-10's trigger. A two-shot burst caught the man full in the face as he straightened up. The bullet impacts and his own momentum carried him over onto his back. He crashed to the floor, legs kicking in spasms of death.

The Executioner took a quick peek out the doorway. Through the still-swirling dust, he could see that the explosion had turned the back side of the staircase into a jumble of heat-scorched plaster and splintered timbers.

No one was coming through that way soon.

For the moment, the Executioner had covered his own rear.

Autofire crackled. Muzzle-flashes winked at him from the right. He jerked back as bullets gnawed at the edge of the door frame.

The opposition had finally arrived, en masse.

Gunfire continued, pinning Bolan inside the room, forcing him to keep his head and weapon down. Over the sound of shooting, he could hear running feet as men moved to take positions behind the other doorways.

The success of the Executioner's mission depended on movement. Free, unencumbered movement. It was the only way he could hit and go. Outnumbered, outgunned, if he allowed himself to be stopped, the enemy would wear him down, run him out of ammo and kill him.

As the shooting outside dwindled, Bolan could hear weak cries for help. On the other side of the building, men were still alive, trapped amid the avalanched stairs.

The Executioner pulled a fragmentation grenade from his combat harness. He drew out the pin and flipped off the grip safety. Bending down, he chucked it around the bottom of the door frame, out into the hall.

He only had a rough idea where the doorways on the other side were located. He wasn't really trying for a hole in one. All he wanted was a lull in the attack.

The grenade detonated in the enclosed space with a hard *whack*. Shrapnel sang through the air, thudding into the corridor walls.

As Bolan popped out around the door, pale cordite smoke was still unfurling from the hallway floor.

At a glance, he picked and sequenced his targets, bracing the MAC-10 against the chewed-up door frame. A guard stood in a room two doors down on the opposite side. He was well back from the corridor, frowning as he tried to see through the smoke. Bolan fired a short burst, aimed dead center at the man's chest. It drove the man backward into the room. He landed with a loud thud.

Bolan swung the MAC-10's stubby muzzle around to target number two.

A guard on his side of the hallway was making frantic hand signals to the others across the way, trying to co-ordinate their attack. The SMG chugged in the Executioner's fist, letting fly another short burst. The impacts of slugs along the guard's arm and shoulder pulled him out of hiding, spinning him into the hall and driving him down on one knee. Bolan quickly followed up with a shot to the back of the man's head. In a puff of red, the guard's uniform cap flew off, along with the top of his skull.

The MAC-10's action locked open.

Out of business.

Bolan drew back to reload the submachine gun, but before he did, he located two more of the opposition. Down at the end of the hallway, close to the elevator shaft, sticking out of opposite doorways, he saw the flash hiders of a pair of assault rifles.

A flurry of gunshots clipped the door frame as he dumped the spent mag and replaced it. The defense seemed a bit less enthusiastic.

Time to rock.

The Executioner pulled two grenades from his harness, a tear gas canister and another fragmentation grenade. He primed the frag, holding the grip safety on, then, during a lull in the firing, pitched the gas grenade into the hallway without pulling its pin. The tear gas canister thudded as it bounced along the middle of the corridor. Bolan was counting on the guards' short-term memory, on their connecting the sight and noise of the small, rolling object with the lethal threat of another antipersonnel device and pulling back for cover.

It worked.

Bolan stepped out into a deserted hallway. The tear gas canister rolled away from him, toward the elevator. As he ran after it, he let the frag's grip safety fly off. Two doors down, on his side of the hall, he had seen one of the remaining guards. As he angled for the closest of the two rooms, he left-handed the grenade through the next door down.

The frag detonated with a solid *crack* as he ducked

into the first doorway. Shards of red-hot steel cut slashes
through the lathe and plaster of the intervening wall.
Bolan immediately turned and looked out into the hallway, which was choked with plaster dust and smoke.
Not ten feet away, a man's body lay facedown on the
tile, with its arms spread. The guard had been blown
from the room as he had tried and failed to dive away
from the grenade's blast. In the middle of his back, running from shoulder blades to hips, there was a huge
bloody crater.

The Executioner waited, his weapon braced against
the doorjamb, sights lined up. Sooner or later, he knew
the surviving guard would have to look out from his
hiding place.

He didn't have to wait long.

When the man peered around the lower half of the
doorway, Bolan dropped his aim and pinned the trigger.
The MAC-10 snarled, spewing a stream of spent brass.
Nine millimeter slugs plucked at the man's shirt, driving
him down, holding him trapped against the door frame
until Bolan let up on the trigger.

The Executioner crossed the corridor on the run, to
make sure the man was down for keeps. The guard lay
on his side, his eyes open, but already glazing over, the
pupils huge and doll-like. A puddle of red spread out
from beneath his body, as blood poured from half a
dozen wounds.

As Bolan looked up from the dead man, he was
greeted by more gunfire, this time from beside the elevator. On the right of the shaft, two muzzles winked
death at him. Slugs slapped the wall above his head,
gouging long furrows in the masonry, showering him
with bits of plaster. He quickly stepped over the corpse
and into the room.

In his mind, the soldier held an image of the end of the hallway. He had measured the distance to the elevator shaft and the angle of the wall beyond it. He unclipped another grenade from his harness, noting that it was the next to the last of his stockpile. When the shooting stopped for a moment, the guards either running out of ammo or clearing jammed actions, Bolan leaned out and underhanded the armed frag. His high lob bounced the live grenade off the floor once, right in front of the shaft, then off the far wall, softly dropping it behind the shooters.

As Bolan drew back, the grenade detonated. The air quaked and bits of hot shrap screamed down the hallway. Debris was still falling from the ceiling as he hurled himself out of the room. The MAC-10 was ready in his fist as he charged the elevator.

But it wasn't needed.

The grenade had caught both guards flat-footed and from the rear. The blast had hurled them into the steel doors of the elevator, and bounced them back to the floor. Neither man was quite dead, but both were horribly wounded, bodies torn and mangled by the close-range explosion. Bolan ended their misery with a contact wound to each of their heads.

On the far side of the shaft was another fifty feet of corridor. It led to an exit doorway much like the one on the other side of the building. A stairwell on the right gave access to the upper floors. The elevator doors faced the exit and the stairs, which meant Bolan would have to work with his back unprotected to the enemy, at least for a brief time.

There was no way around it.

He put down his weapons and dropped the second satchel to the floor beside them. Then he drew his

SEAL-2000 knife from its sheath, jamming the point between the closed doors, using it to lever them apart and get a grip on their inside edges. With his fingertips in place, Bolan strained mightily to separate the doors. When he had them a yard apart, he wedged his body between them.

Looking down the shaft, directly below him, he could see the roof of the car, which was stopped on the next floor. Bolan reached up with the heavy knife and stabbed it into the overhead track the doors ran on, which kept one of the doors from completely closing. Then a motor whirred to life and the set of cables before him started to move. The elevator car dropped away, descending into darkness.

At that instant, a dozen shots rang out from the foot of the staircase. Bullets spanged into the elevator shaft, gouging quarter-size holes in the metal doors. Bolan twisted out from between them and lunged for his weapons.

CAPTAIN SUAREZ was watching his men's faces as again and again explosions went off over their heads. The guards cringed at the sounds, gripping their weapons for dear life.

Though he had trained his men to face such dangers, mere exercises couldn't convey the mindless frenzy and randon mayhem of actual combat. The idea of grenades exploding in small, enclosed spaces, of an enemy willing to use such unselective weapons, had struck home to his troops that any or all of them could die this day.

The important thing, Captain Suarez knew, was to keep their minds in the game, to not let them dwell on the danger. If they did, they would be paralyzed, and they would lose. Both the gold and their lives.

Cebollo lowered his walkie-talkie. He leaned close to Suarez' ear and spoke in a soft voice so the others couldn't hear the news. "I have confirmation that the intruders have penetrated to the elevator shaft, and that we have taken heavy casualties," he said. "The front of the building is in ruins and no longer accessible to the men on the upper stories. With the main stairs collapsed, there is no way for us to outflank the enemy. We have no choice but to take them head-on."

Suarez showed no emotion, no weakness. He knew it was conceivable, perhaps even likely that his men would lose control of the elevator. That the battle would spill into the lower floors.

Suarez picked five men from the ranks and waved them over to the elevator. To Cebollo he said, "You're in command of the garrison. I'm taking these men down to the depository. At all costs, you must maintain control of the shaft."

He stepped into the car with the others and pressed the button for the bottom floor. With a lurch, they began their descent. Outwardly, Suarez radiated total confidence in his contingency plans and in the ability of his men to execute them. Inside, however, cracks were beginning to form.

Suarez knew that with sufficiently heavy explosives, such as those that had already been used against the depository, the intruders could put a quick end to the battle. There was no defense against such overwhelming force, which left the captain thinking less about the safety of the drug lord's gold and more about his own immediate survival.

When the elevator car reached the bottom floor, Suarez ordered his men out, then he opened the control panel and disabled the car. It wouldn't rise again until he wanted it to.

The gold storeroom level was fitted with a built-in bunker. Its machine gun port commanded the elevator, turning it into a point-blank killzone. Beyond the low bunker, along the walls of the large room, were niches. Each niche had a floor-to-ceiling steel mesh doorway. Through the mesh, the pallets of gold bars were visible, stacked as high as a man's head.

Safely behind the bunker's reinforced concrete walls, Suarez took a red telephone from the cradle on the back wall. There was no dial; it was a direct line. He dreaded making the call, but he had no choice. It was protocol.

Samosa had to be notified.

DUCKING THE HAIL of autofire, Mack Bolan swept up his satchel and one of the submachine guns and dived around the corner of the elevator shaft. He had reached safety but he was cut off from the elevator doors. For him to proceed, the gunfire had to stop, at least momentarily.

A quick look around the corner told the Executioner that he faced four more men, clustered inside the entrance to the stairwell. With concentrated gunfire, they forced him to pull his head back. In a few seconds, they would realize what the situation was. That there was only one of him. And then, under covering fire, a couple of them would advance to the other side of the shaft. If they got that close he was in big trouble.

He yanked his last fragmentation grenade from the harness and pulled the pin. When the volume of the gunfire suddenly dropped, he knew the opposition was making its move. He let the grenade's grip safety flip off, waited three seconds, then pitched the bomb around the corner.

The explosion shook the floor under his feet, dropped part of the ceiling and sent chunks of plaster bounding down the hallway.

Bolan poked the muzzle of the MAC-10 around the corner into the choking, caustic smoke. Two men were facedown on the floor, the backs of their clothing on fire. The shooting from the stairs had stopped as the guards standing there had ducked back to avoid flying shrapnel.

They'd dashed back up the steps, but not far enough, as it turned out.

Bolan pinned the Ingram's trigger, pouring slugs into the stairwell entrance. The torrent of lead pounded one of the men into the staircase before he could bring his weapon to bear. Bolan swung the muzzle, walking bullets across the man who crouched above him. Stitched with 9 mm rounds, the second guy twisted sideways, clutched for the stair railing, missed it, then fell headfirst down the stairs. Both men toppled down the steps, spraying blood and screaming.

The MAC-10 barked until their cries were stilled.

Knowing that his window of opportunity was narrow, the Executioner rushed around the side of the shaft with the satchel in hand. Jerking the arming cord, he slung the bag down the elevator shaft.

It landed with a thud on the roof of the car below.

As he turned to scoop up the fully loaded SMG he'd left on the floor, autofire clipped the edges of the elevator shaft, sailing past and slamming into the exit door in front of him. It was coming from the other side of the building. The upstairs guards had managed to circumvent the fallen staircase and enter the hallway from the other end. They were pouring withering fire into the corridor.

The Executioner didn't shoot back. There wasn't time. The elevator shaft offered him, at best, momentary cover from the rear attack. The guards were advancing on the run, trying to get into position to angle their shots around the sides to nail him. Soon they would be able to do it. He only had one chance, and that was the door to the outside. He sprinted for it.

Twenty feet from the exit, the satchel detonated with a roar behind him. A blistering wind rushed out of the elevator shaft, gusting over his back, enveloping him in smoke and flying debris. Bolan didn't break stride. He had already ripped the remote detonator from his combat harness. With a flip of his thumb, he armed it.

9

Eight security guards stared at Ernesto Rodriguez, awaiting orders. They looked nervous, shocked, as if suddenly awakened from a deep sleep.

He screamed at his men to get their full attention and, in so doing, released a very small part of the anger he felt at the violation of the perimeter and the mansion, at the insult to his honor and the honor of his garrison.

Rodriguez split his force, sending the sniper teams to opposite ends of the building, then, on the run, he led the rest of the men to the entrance to the stairs leading down from the roof. Approaching it, he drew his side arm, a blue-steel Browning Hi-Power. As his hand closed on the doorknob, the first satchel charge exploded beneath and behind them.

The supporting rafters snapped, and a yawning pit opened. For an instant Rodriguez thought the whole roof was going to fall in. As a torrent of dust and smoke billowed up from the widening hole, at the wall's edge huge beams sheared off, one after another, dominoes falling, while he stood there, caught like a deer in the headlights.

As the section of roof Rodriguez and his men were standing on began to tip downward, the guards at the back of the pack had to throw themselves forward, scrambling to avoid being drawn into the hole.

Through the boiling smoke, Rodriguez could no longer see the snipers he'd sent to the far side of the roof. They had either retreated to safety against the edge of the front wall or had been sucked into the collapse.

"Come on!" he shouted at the men who surrounded him. He jerked open the metal door and charged down the stairs with his 9 mm autoloader out in front in a two-handed grip.

Ahead of them, there were no lights. The hallway was shrouded in a coarse, gritty fog of dust and smoke. As they advanced into it, the cloud became so thick that Rodriguez had to tie a bandanna over his nose and mouth to keep from choking.

After going another fifteen or twenty feet, they came to an avalanche of ceiling and roof that completely blocked the hallway. They couldn't reach the stairwell at the front of the mansion.

"Shit!" he said. He swiveled and pushed roughly past his men, leading them back the way they'd come, out of the smoke.

As they ran, a few other guards who'd survived the explosion staggered from rooms along the corridor. Rodriguez shouted for the dazed men to bring up the rear.

Halfway down the hall, he turned into a room on the left and sprinted for its blast-emptied window frames. Just outside the tattered gauzy curtains was a metal fire escape. As Rodriguez stuck a leg out over the window sash, more autofire rattled from the ground floor. It was followed by the hard crack of a detonating hand grenade.

No one on Rodriguez's side had been issued hand grenades, which meant the robbers were using them to soften resistance and ease their way to the elevator. In enclosed, tight quarters, he knew there was no defense against such a vicious attack. If he was to do any good, he had to hurry.

Rodriguez scrambled out the window and onto the fire escape landing. With the rest of the men following closely behind, he scrambled down the tiers of rickety steel ladders. As he jumped to the ground, another grenade exploded, followed by the unmistakable, canvas-ripping sound of a high-rate-of-fire submachine gun.

Unanswered enemy fire.

Without waiting for the others to join him, Rodriguez moved toward the open doorway. To reach it, he had to step over the body of a guard. He didn't bother to check the man for signs of life; at a glance he knew there would be none. The guard lay on his back on the floor in a pool of gore. The middle of his chest had three tightly spaced bullet holes in it.

Another grenade exploded outside the room. He instinctively drew back as shrapnel screamed down the hall, past the doorway, from left to right. The battle for the elevator was already almost lost.

Rodriguez waited a second, gathering himself for the charge. Behind him, the rest of the guards were pouring in through the window. From his position he could see what remained of the mansion's stately branching staircase. Everything beautiful was gone. In its place was a trash heap, a floor-to-ceiling avalanche of shattered wood and plaster.

For an instant, there was a lull in the shooting. He heard the moaning from the other side of the collapsed staircase. Men were still alive, caught in the debris and calling out weakly for help.

"Come on!" he shouted at the guards lined up behind him. And with that, he rushed out into the hall. The lieutenant was pumped, ready, eager to kill, but in the corridor in front of him he could see no one. No one alive. The scattered bodies were all guards. The air was thick with the smell of cordite and burning flesh. The walls were stained with blast residue and sprayed blood. On the far side of the elevator shaft, someone was still shooting.

Rodriguez opened fire as he ran, shooting blindly at the corners of the elevator shaft. His men followed suit, shooting their G-3s from the hip. When there was no immediate return of fire, Rodriguez had a glimmer of hope. Perhaps they had caught the attackers off guard, perhaps they could trap the enemy or drive them out of the building before they descended the elevator shaft.

As Rodriguez veered to the right, trying for a wider shooting angle, the satchel charge in the elevator shaft detonated. It rocked the floor so suddenly, so violently, that it seemed to jump up and smash him in the face. He refused to stay down, but scrambled up at once, tasting blood in his mouth.

What happened next was inconceivable.

From behind, Rodriguez felt an impossible pressure and heat. Though he was moving forward, lunging for the elevator, he sensed he was falling backward. For a nanosecond his body withstood the horrendous force.

Then he was gone.

The shock wave of the armored car bomb blew him apart, his vaporized remains mixing with splinters and plaster dust. Ernesto Rodriguez became one with the trash heap.

As BOLAN full-out charged the mansion's exit doors, he got a glimpse of a brown face and the muzzle of an assault rifle. Some of the guards had circled the building and were coming at him from this side.

A yard from the exit, he triggered the armored car's detonator.

His next stride was a long one.

The explosion's shock wave lifted and hurled him through the gaping doors and out of the building. The guard standing on the other side of the exit took the brunt of Bolan's weight crashing into him and was bowled over backward. Stunned by the impact himself, Bolan belly flopped down the flight of marble steps, as clouds of smoke and dirt washed over him.

Choking, he pushed to his feet.

A great black pyre rose from the ruined building, but the demolition wasn't over, yet. As he backed away, part of the side wall gave way, huge blocks of stone tumbling into the bomb crater.

Tumbling in silence.

The Executioner realized then that he'd been blast-deafened. It felt like his head had been stuffed with cotton.

Movement from the building above him caught his attention and he looked up. He saw boot soles and kicking legs. A guard hung by one hand from the ledge of a third-story window, perhaps blown part way through it by the force of the explosion. Bolan moved out of the way as the guard let go and dropped, waving his arms wildly to keep an upright position. Upright or headfirst, with a fall from that height it really didn't matter. The guard bounced as he hit the flagstones. He didn't get up.

As Bolan turned away, showers of sparks leaped from the staircase behind him. It was aimed fire. The Executioner looked for the source. It was coming from many angles at once, and it was blocking his way out.

He had to move.

Move now or die.

WHEN THE ARMORED car bomb exploded, Captain Suarez was sitting in the depository bunker behind sandbag barricades, waiting for his call to Don Jorge Samosa to cycle through its scramble links. The pressure on his ears made him scream. A scream lost in the roar as the building caved in on itself. The floors above him pancaked as they were driven downward by the force of the blast. Most of the ceiling came crashing down, too.

One second he was fine; the next, his body had been flattened to the floor and was being securely held in an agonizing position. It was all he could do to breathe with the terrible weight pressing down on his chest and the smothering dust. He fought to stay conscious. Gradually, he became aware of a tickling sensation down the sides of his neck. Blood was flowing freely from his ears.

He tried to move his legs but couldn't budge them. He was only able to move his right arm. As he did, he brushed something in the dark with his fingertips. Something warm and wet. He recognized the shape of a human face. Groaning, he jerked his hand back.

"Is anybody else alive?" he said. "Can anybody hear me?"

No one answered.

It was then that Suarez noticed a spreading coolness beneath him. At first he thought he'd wet himself, but reaching down he knew that wasn't the case. There was water on the floor of the collapsed bunker. It was streaming from broken pipes somewhere, pooling at the mansion's lowest point. Given the rate of flow, it would soon fill the subbasement.

With a shock, the captain realized that he was probably going to drown before any rescuers found him.

Summoning all his strength, Suarez opened his mouth and began to shriek for help.

To his own ears, it sounded like a baby crying.

10

When the armored car blew, Lico Tejeda and Alberto Gomez were crouched at opposite ends of the museum's roof, their G-3 SG/1 Heckler & Koch police sniper rifles braced against the roofline's embrasures, waiting for targets to appear.

The shock wave slammed them into the wall and bounced them onto their backs on the roof. Tejeda opened his eyes and saw dark specks high in the sky above him, specks falling through a curtain of gray. Tejeda gasped and rolled to his stomach as the first of the chunks of masonry crashed to the roof. He covered the back of his head with his hands and curled into a ball. Pieces of debris, some the size of basketballs, rained on the rooftop and a plume of black smoke swept over his position.

Beneath his belly, the roof rippled as if it was made of water. For what seemed like an eternity, bits of the building continued to fall, screaming down at him from a tremendous height. After a few seconds, the chunks got smaller, then they stopped altogether. When Tejeda struggled up, he saw that the front of the building had vanished. A vast crater was all that remained. The short section that was left of the roof angled steeply down into the boiling smoke.

Gunfire erupted from the mansion's back gardens,

which were spread out before him. Bullets smashed into the building's facade. Tejeda grabbed the sniper rifle that he had dropped. At first he thought it was more of the intruders, shooting at him as they penetrated the rear gates. But then he realized that the impacts were three stories below.

As Tejeda raised his head above the level of the embrasure, Gomez scurried up to him. "Let's get out of here," he said. "The building's on fire." He gave Tejeda a firm nudge toward the fire escape ladder.

Gomez's nose was a bloody mess, trickles ran around his mustache and dripped off the end of his chin.

"Not yet," Tejeda told him. "These bastards killed many of our friends. They have to pay for that." He poked his rifle out over the edge of the roof, peering over the top of the telescopic sight. "There's one of them!" he cried. He put his eye to the scope, swinging the G-3 at a tall figure running away from them. The man was dashing for the line of trees that bordered the long driveway. Between the intruder and the gates, guards had taken positions behind the stonework of the ornamental fountains, firing at the running man.

For Tejeda, the shooting angle was bad.

Aiming from such a height meant that the target was reduced to just head and shoulders, bobbing head and shoulders. Tejeda had to wait until the man was farther away.

Meanwhile, Gomez was looking warily over his shoulder at the smoke, wincing at the heat billowing up from the gutted part of the structure.

"We have time to nail this one," Tejeda said with confidence. "All we need is one more minute."

Gomez grunted and swung up his own rifle. Using the embrasure as a gun rest, he flipped up the caps on his telescopic sight and snugged the buttstock into his shoulder.

"Get ready to shoot," Tejeda told Gomez, "as soon as the bastard gets past the fountains."

THE EXECUTIONER made no attempt to return fire; to do so effectively, he would have had to stop running. And under the circumstances, to stop before he reached cover would have been suicide. There were too many guns shooting at him. He counted at least three from behind the fountains, a couple more from behind the trunks of the row of trees and another two shooting from the rear gate, his exit of choice, which lay a hundred yards away.

Unfortunately, he couldn't travel in a straight line. He had to skirt the curve of the drive and get behind the trees.

As Bolan sprinted, he saw a man move away from the side of the fountain closest to him. The gunner quickly knelt and took careful aim. With his target running almost right at him, the guard figured to take the easy knockdown shot.

The Executioner pinned his SMG's trigger, fanning the side of the fountain and the kneeling man with a stream of 9 mm slugs. The burst was barely aimed because he was running, but the saturation job did the trick. The guard went down hard, absorbing head and chest hits. The shooting from the other side of the fountain stopped as the men ducked for cover.

Bullets fired from farther on, near the rear gates, skipped off the paving stones all around him. Perhaps because the guards were nervous, or perhaps because they weren't good shots, none of the bullets struck him. He dodged behind the cover of a massive tree trunk.

Slugs whacked into the far side of the tree, clipping off chunks of bark, leaves and small limbs.

The shooting slowed immediately. They were no longer volleys of automatic fire, but single shots, carefully aimed. The opposition was trying to keep him pinned until they could get an angle on him.

Bolan had already discarded the perimeter wall as an escape route. It was too high to climb quickly.

Peering around the tree, he saw movement near the fountains. The guards were advancing, closing ranks so they could concentrate fire on him.

Bolan ripped a CS grenade from his harness, primed it, then popped out from cover long enough to lob it sidearm. The gas bomb arced high, landing ten feet in front of the guards and upwind of the fountain. It exploded with a bang and hiss.

Clouds of white smoke whipped over the gunmen's position. Without protective gear, they were blinded in seconds. Coughing, gasping, they tried to retreat from under the stinging blanket of gas.

As he dashed for the next tree, Bolan fired from the hip, sweeping a line of bullets through the staggering men. As the breeze pushed the CS aside, he saw three of them jerk and twist. The burst of hot lead drove one of the guards to his knees, then over onto his side, clutching at his stomach. The second man toppled headfirst into the fountain, sending a wave of water splashing over the rim. The third man managed to belly-crawl around the base of the fountain, dragging his nowuseless legs behind him and leaving a wide trail of smeared blood.

His flank now safe from attack, Bolan raced for the next tree. As he did so, his body was slammed by a tremendous impact that twisted him and drove him to the ground. He lay there, face in the dirt, unable to breathe or move his legs. If he hadn't known better, he'd have thought he'd been blindsided by a truck.

From across the compound came shouts and the sound of running feet coming toward him.

HOLDING THE SCOPE'S centerpost in a stationary lead on the running target, Lico Tejeda released the sniper rifle's trigger.

Sixty yards downrange, the tall man went down, hard.

"Got the fucker!" Tejeda cried.

His words were lost in the roar of Gomez' rifle.

Through his scope, Tejeda saw the second bullet's impact. It missed the back of the downed man's arm by no more than an inch, gouging a hole in the sod and kicking up a sizable divot.

"You missed him," Tejeda laughed.

"Shit."

"Aim for the head," Tejeda said, once again tucking the G-3 tight into his shoulder. He put the scope's sight post on the base of the intruder's neck.

"Got it," Gomez said.

"On the count of three," Tejeda told him. "One, two, three...."

WHEN THE HEAVY-CALIBER slug freight-trained into the ground beside him, Bolan could feel the shudder of its impact right through the earth.

Sure as hell more follow-ups were coming.

He fought to beat back the paralyzing numbness that still gripped him. He'd taken a midtorso bullet strike. His armored vest had saved his life. The down-angled rifle slug had skipped off the trauma plate over his kidneys. The steel insert could reflect a high-powered bullet and keep it from penetrating his body, but it couldn't absorb a thousand pounds of force. It was the shock of the deflection that had pounded his face into the dirt and made him lose all feeling in his legs. From the angle of fire, he figured that the shooters were on top of the depository.

If he waited any longer, he was never going to get up.

Summoning his strength, he rolled to his right. At the same instant, a pair of gunshots rang out. Slugs ripped into the ground where his head had just been. Scrambling to his feet, he used the overhead branches as cover as he ran for the next tree trunk.

Bullets screamed down through the branches, wide of the mark.

Too little too late.

As he reached the safety of the tree, he stamped his feet to get rid the last of the tingling sensation in his legs. Ahead, he could see trouble. A gap between the last of the trees and the rear gates would give the snipers on the roof of the museum clear shots at him. Forty feet of golden opportunity to nail him for real. They needed to be discouraged from firing at him.

The trouble was, making an accurate shot, up-angled and from this distance, was going to be tough. Drawing the Beretta and cocking the exposed hammer, Bolan dropped into a crouch and moved away from the trunk until he could see the top of the building and the roofline through the leaves and branches.

At a sixty-degree angle above him, in side-by-side shooting rests were two heads behind two scoped rifles. Holding low to compensate for the angle, the Executioner squeezed off a single shot.

The bullet made a thwacking sound as it hit. A solid thwack.

The head he had aimed at, the one on the left, disappeared from view. A second later, the head on the right disappeared, too.

His rear no longer under threat, Bolan raced around the far side of the tree.

As Bolan holstered the Beretta and reloaded both MAC-10s with full mags, he felt a burning sensation in his eyes. The breeze had pushed the edge of the tear gas cloud his way. Farther downwind, the men in the guard hut that stood beside the gate were taking the brunt of the drifting tear gas. From the way their bullets were missing the tree trunk, the guards were having trouble seeing.

There was only one way to test the theory, of course.

The Executioner broke from cover.

TEJEDA GROWLED a curse the instant his rifle's trigger broke—he knew it was going to be a miss. Through the scope he watched the tall man roll to the right. Both his and Gomez's shots went wide.

"Get him!" Tejeda said, swinging his sights up, tracking the target as it glided beneath the overhanging branches. He fired three more times, leading the moving shape behind the screen of tree limbs. Whether the bullets were deflected by the branches or pulled off target by Tejeda's haste, the man reached the cover of the next tree.

"Do you see him?" Alberto Gomez asked. "Where did he go?"

Both men searched the area with their telescopic sights. Tejeda caught a glimpse of something moving at the base of the tree. "There!" he cried.

Before he could line up the shot, a single gun crack rang out.

Beside him, Gomez jolted, his head snapping back, chin pointing at the sky, rifle falling free from his grasp.

Pulling back from the notch, Tejeda moved to help his friend. There was a very large hole in the top of his head.

Tejeda felt the heat of fire at his back. Flames were licking through the rubble. Though he wanted to get off another shot, he couldn't stay. He had to get off the roof.

As Tejeda ran for the fire escape, he skated on the steaming-hot tar paper and liquified asphalt.

Thin ice, as it turned out.

With a loud crack, the roof gave way under his weight and he fell through it, into a three-story inferno.

AUTOMATIC FIRE coming from the guardhouse and the rear gate drove Bolan behind the last tree in the line. From inside the guard hut, two men fired erratically in his direction. Another guard, perhaps less troubled by the drift of the initial tear gas, shot more accurately from between the bars of the gate.

As the Executioner jerked the last CS canister from his harness, over his shoulder he saw the flames leaping from the depository's roof. No more snipers to worry about up there. He primed the grenade and sidearmed it around the tree. Then he gripped a MAC-10 in each hand and dropped the selector switches to full auto.

The canister popped, and thick white smoke poured out, drifting through the gate and over the guard hut. The Executioner stepped out from behind the cover of the tree. Before him, the guardhouse was half hidden in smoke; the gate completely obscured by it. None of the three men he had marked were visible.

Not until he got within twenty feet.

Whether they heard him coming or whether they just

couldn't stand the burn of the CS any longer, the guards jumped up with assault rifles blazing. Faces reddened, blind eyes full of fear, they were fighting for their lives.

The Executioner fired both SMG's at once, streaming lead through the hut's empty window frames. The guards inside were slammed backward by dozens of hits. The muzzles of their weapons climbed out of control, firing into the ceiling even as they dropped out of sight.

As the CS smoke drifted, something moved on each side of the gate. As he swung the MAC-10s around, an automatic rifle stuttered and a flurry of bullets whizzed past his head. The double submachine guns chugged in Bolan's fists, slugs singing off the steel gate, whacking into the gatepost.

The shooter pulled back, behind the solid perimeter wall.

Bolan couldn't tell if he'd hit the guy or not. But he thought not. He advanced to the gate quickly, ready to follow up with more Parabellums. As he pulled back the gate, he heard the sound of someone running down the alley on the far side of the wall.

The Executioner slipped through the gate, his weapons ready. Around the corner, an assault rifle lay discarded in the middle of the road. Sure enough, to his left, a man in uniform was sprinting full-tilt.

From the direction of downtown San José, police and fire sirens could be heard. It was time to go.

As he started trotting away, he began off-loading nonessential gear. Gear that would bring unwanted attention to him. He tossed both MAC-10s over the depository's perimeter wall. Pulling the Beretta from the shoulder holster, he let the empty combat harness drop to the ground behind him. Then he unfastened the velcro straps of his body armor and let it fall, too. It hurt some as he breathed. His chest had taken a severe beating. He figured he'd be lucky to get away without some cracked ribs.

He unscrewed the Beretta's sound suppressor and put it in his pocket, slipping the pistol under his untucked shirt at the small of his back.

The sirens were getting closer; he picked up the pace.

Something heavy hit the ground behind him, beside the museum's wall.

"Stop!" a man's voice cried at his back.

The Executioner froze.

"Turn around and raise your hands," the voice said in Spanish.

"You're making a mistake," Bolan said as he faced the man.

The guard held a shouldered assault rifle, its muzzle pointing at Bolan's unprotected chest. "No mistake," he said, grinning fiercely.

From the way the guy was standing, the tension in his shoulders, the braced stance, Bolan knew he was about to shoot. He sidestepped in a blur, faster than the guard could track, and dropped into a crouch. The assault rifle chattered, firing high and wide. Bolan's right hand came out from behind his back. The 93-R cracked once.

A snap shot.

The guard took the round in the solar plexus. Grimacing, he folded and crashed to the ground.

"Sit still and you'll live," Bolan said, kicking the G-3 out of the wounded man's reach. "Help will be here in a couple of minutes."

With that, he replaced the Beretta under his shirt and jogged quickly away.

11

San Diego, 10:05 a.m.

Hal Brognola rode alone in the rear seat of the unmarked Justice car, bone-tired and stiff-backed. The little sleep he'd managed to catch on the plane from Mexico City had done him more harm than good. His head felt thick, foggy. Not the best state of mind to be in when conducting an important and sensitive interview, but he had no choice.

There was always coffee, he told himself. Lots and lots of coffee.

The Justice driver bypassed the freeway, which was locked bumper to bumper heading out of downtown, and took the city streets, instead. He paralleled Interstate 5, following the base of the hills facing west that overlooked the airport and San Diego Bay.

After traveling a couple of miles, they crossed under the freeway, then angled up a steep, broad street. At the top of the mesa, he turned off onto a palm tree–lined boulevard. It wound through a neighborhood of large homes. They were spaced close together and immaculately maintained.

They pulled into a driveway blocked by high, steel, motorized gates. The house beyond was hidden by tall, stuccoed walls. The gates rolled back, allowing the Justice car to enter a small, secure parking area beside a black Suburban. The gates closed behind them.

Agent Madeline De Leo met Brognola at the front door. She looked beat, but she managed a bright smile of greeting.

"How are they doing?" the big Fed asked her as he stepped through the doorway, into the coolness of the house.

"The real shock of their loss is starting to set in, I'm afraid," she told him. "Both boys seem more frightened now than they were a day or two ago. That's probably the reason for Juanito's nightmares. He and Pedro are starting to withdraw. That's to be expected, though. Textbook trauma reaction. I doubt that you're going to get direct confirmation of what we talked about earlier."

Brognola doubted it, too. But he had to try. Even something indirect, an unguarded look, a careless gesture, might tell him what he needed to know. The other normal avenues of investigation had turned up more suspicions, but nothing remotely conclusive. The boys' original birth certificates had been checked. There was no father listed on them, only the mother's name. Which was strange, since the man who was supposed to be their father was a well-known public figure who had never denied the paternity. It was also strange that, from all accounts, the Mexican television actor never had anything to do with the boys' lives.

"What's your opinion on the best way to conduct the interviews?" he asked De Leo.

"Push either boy too hard," she said, "and they'll stop talking. It's almost like a conditioned response with these kids. They both understand there is a reason for keeping quiet, and they say as little as possible in answer to direct questions. Their mother must have instilled that kind of caution in them, early on. I haven't been able to get any more details out of Juanito. When I ask him about his nightmares, he gives me a blank look. And all I've gotten out of his brother are denials. Though I've been careful not to confront them directly with anything, my poking around the issue has turned them cold to me.''

Brognola wasn't surprised. He'd known this wasn't going to be easy. ''I'll talk to the older one first,'' he said. ''Alone.''

Agent De Leo led him through a pair of French doors and out onto a flagstone patio. The sun reflecting off the white rock was painfully bright. Reaching inside his suit jacket, Brognola took out a pair of sunglasses and put them on.

Beside a covered hot tub, two young boys were playing intently with a fleet of plastic trucks. In one corner of the deck was a small cabana. A black steel fence, ten feet high, set in a low brick wall, formed the back border of the property. Beyond the fence, the landscape dropped away precipitously. Brognola stepped to the edge of the fence and looked down.

The deck overhung a steep canyon, choked with vegetation. To create a fire buffer, the undergrowth directly downslope had been cleared for a distance of twenty yards. To the left, six or seven hundred feet down and a quarter mile away, the mouth of the canyon opened onto Highway 8 and Mission Valley.

Brognola knew that the sides of the canyon wouldn't stop an attack, but they'd make for mighty slow going. Because of the way the safehouse was angled on its lot, there was no direct line of sight from the houses on the opposite side of the canyon rim. The only straight shot was from clear across Mission Valley, and that was probably a mile away. The Justice sentries on watch out-side stood in the shade or sat under the patio table's striped umbrella. Shoulder-slung machine pistols were ready for immediate use as they intermittently scanned the downhill slopes with massive pairs of binoculars.

Brognola took a seat on a bench near the boys, but in the shade. He took off his sunglasses so the children could see his eyes.

"Pedro and Juanito," De Leo said, "do you remem-ber Mr. Bernett?" she asked, using Brognola's alias. "He's here to talk to you."

They ignored him.

"Juanito, come with me," De Leo said cheerily. "We need some help in the kitchen. Conchita is making a surprise for lunch."

The younger boy looked at his brother expectantly. It was not as if he was asking for permission to go, but to indicate that he was worried about leaving him in a stranger's company.

Pedro resumed playing with his trucks, apparently un-concerned by the big Fed's looming presence.

Brognola was already getting a sense of the nature of the boys' relationship. It was more than just tight. While they were playing, there had been none of the usual sib-ling squabbling. They were a unit. A defensive team. They had been operating that way for a long time.

Brognola sat on the bench, watching the older boy play for a moment, then he said, "I need to ask you a few questions, son. They're important."

Pedro glanced up from his truck. "What's going to happen to me and my brother?" he said.

Brognola hesitated, wondering if he should tell the boy the truth, part of the truth or none of the truth. A devoted father himself, it was difficult for him not to project his feelings for his own children into the situation. If what Juanito had said in his sleep had been interpreted correctly by De Leo, the implications were serious and far-reaching. If it was true, the boys were going to need a much higher level of government protection for a very long time. If it was true, they were going to be an invaluable asset in the all-out campaign against Don Jorge Samosa. They were going to be leverage.

"We'll take care of you," Brognola said, and he meant it.

"My brother and I don't want your help," Pedro told him. "We don't want to stay here. We want to go back to Mexico."

"Why's that, son?"

"Because it's our home."

"But you've got no one down there to look after you, anymore. And you're in danger."

The boy was adamant. "We want to go home. You have no right to keep us here."

Whether the boy realized it or not, the latter statement was legally accurate. Brognola had no right to detain them in the United States. Yovana Ortiz's sons were Mexican citizens.

The big Fed had thought long and hard about what he was about to say. And whether he should say it at all. His problem was time: it was running out. If he waited to gain the boy's confidence, perhaps spending days or weeks at it, he still might come up empty. If Pedro and Juanito were Samosa's sons, he'd want them back. Chances were that he was already looking for them. In which case, Brognola's keeping them in San Diego wasn't a good idea. Sooner or later, someone would give them up. With the amount of money the drug lord had to wave around, with the kind of intimidation he could buy, he would eventually locate his children. The tip didn't have to come from a corrupt federal agent. It could come from a neighbor or the mailman. For all Brognola knew, Samosa had already acquired a list of Bureau safehouses and he was checking them out, one by one. With these hazards well in mind, Brognola took the plunge.

"You want to go back to your father, don't you?" he said.

Pedro resumed playing with his truck. He really leaned on it, grinding the plastic wheels into the deck.

"We know who your real father is," Brognola went on. "Your real father, not your pretend father."

The boy's head jerked up.

"I know you love him, but he's a bad man," Brognola said. "A very bad man. We think he's the one who hurt your mother. He hurt her because she was helping the United States government."

"Shut up! Shut up!" the boy shouted at him.

The big Fed leaned down. "Believe me, I'm not saying these things to be mean to you," he said in a soothing tone of voice. "I'm saying them because you and I need to work together to protect your brother. Juanito's not big enough to understand what the consequences are, here, but you are. You know if we're not very careful, things could get real bad." Brognola leaned closer to the boy, and in an even softer voice said, "Pedro, everything bad that's happened to you has happened because your father is Don Jorge Luis Samosa."

"That's a lie!"

"That's the truth, Pedro. You and I both know it. I promise you, nobody is going to let your secret get out. Look me in the eye, son. I'm not lying to you. I want

to help you. You're a very brave boy, but you can't deal
with this by yourself. Your father has enemies who will
hurt you and your brother. They will try to use you to
hurt your father. I need you to tell me the truth about
this, once and for all, so we can make arrangements for
you and Juanito to be safe, always.''

"You don't know anything!" Pedro cried. "And you
can't protect anybody. You were supposed to be protecting our mama.''

The boy was getting more and more distraught.

"Look," Brognola said, "you've got a reason to trust
us. We moved you here to keep you safe, didn't we?
Well, we will move you again, and no one bad will ever
find you. You'll have a new family that will take care
of you and your little brother.''

"We don't want a new family. We want to go home.''

The big Fed took out a handkerchief and dabbed at
the beads of sweat that had surfaced on his brow. It was
hot, even in the shade. As far as direct information, the
interview was going nowhere, fast. Brognola could see
that it was going to take something much more dramatic
to crack the boy's story. The trouble was, all of the dramatic stuff—the threats, the psychological tricks, the
physical intimidation—was way off-limits when it came
to interrogating a child.

Brognola sat there in silence. Did he really expect the
boy to give up his own father? To hand over his closest
surviving relative on a plate? Did he really expect Pedro
to believe what he'd said about who was behind his
mother's murder? The answers to all of the above was
no.

Given the self-imposed limitations on his interrogation
technique, given the extensive training the boys had received from their mother, the best Brognola could hope

for was a contradicting rationale, an explanation that would deny the truth of the Samosa paternity. But Pedro hadn't offered anything in the way of a counterstory, hadn't even thrown out the name of his pretend father, the TV actor, as a shield. That seemed strange to Brognola. It was counterintuitive. All the boy had to say was, "No, so-and-so is my father." Instead, he had clammed up. Perhaps Yovana Ortiz had warned her sons not to offer any information to anyone, for fear of being trapped by a slip of the tongue.

Based on the boy's unusual reaction and on the slaughter that had taken place at the supposed safehouse in Tijuana a few days earlier, Brognola had reason enough to get the kids the hell out of there. Samosa had proved that he was willing to apply any level of force, men and weapons to get his way. And his foot soldiers weren't just run-of-the-mill drug thugs. The Murillos had built a paramilitary-style organization, capable of enforcing the drug lord's will up and down Baja.

Brognola had thought that he had come prepared for this interview, that the tragedy of Pedro and Juanito, the perverse melodrama of father killing mother, couldn't touch him. But sitting there, looking into the boy's face, he knew that it had. And he asked himself which was worse, that these children never found out the truth about their mother's murder or that they did? That they returned to their father, trusting him, when he had robbed them so horribly, or that they shunned him, hated him for the rest of their lives?

The big Fed wasn't a judge or a philosopher. He couldn't begin to answer those questions. A highly skilled and experienced law-enforcement bureaucrat, he could only look at the short-term bottom line. The boys' safety came first, then their value to the operation. He didn't need to talk to the younger boy, right then. He had seen enough to make his decision.

"Why can't you just leave us alone?" Pedro said, tearfully.

"By law, we can't do that," Brognola told him. "You're not old enough to be on your own. No matter where you are, someone has to take care of you. An adult."

Abandoning his trucks, Pedro got up from the deck and walked into the house.

Interview over.

Brognola followed the boy into the kitchen, where Agent De Leo and Juanito were washing vegetables on the center island counter. Juanito was standing on a stool so he could reach the sink.

A Mexican woman in her late-forties, dressed in a white uniform, her black hair wrapped in a bun and covered with a hair net, stood at the oven. She picked up a roast and put it in a heavy pot. Then she added other ingredients from a cutting board: chopped almonds, tomatoes, onion, garlic, diced apples, cinnamon, cloves.

To De Leo, the woman said, "This must cook very slowly with the cover on. You don't have to add any water. It will be ready in three hours."

The cook seemed more than a little distraught. Brognola watched as she dropped her stirring spoon on the floor. Bending down to pick it up, she knocked over a small jar, scattering raisins across the stovetop.

"Oh, I'm sorry," she said.

"Don't worry about it," De Leo said. "I'll get the raisins. You'd better go now, or you'll miss your bus."

"Thank you," the cook said. As she hurried from the kitchen, she untied her apron.

Brognola gave De Leo a questioning look.

"Conchita's leaving early today to go to the doctor," she told him. "She's had some laboratory tests done and she's scared to death to hear the results. Thinks she's got the big *C*."

"Whatever she's making in there," Brognola said, pointing at the pot, "it sure smells mighty good."

"Piccadillo beef," Juanito announced. "It's my favorite."

"Why don't you boys go back outside now?" De Leo said. "Put on some shorts. And ask one of the agents to take the cover off the hot tub so you can play in the water. Tell them I said it was okay."

After the boys had left the room, Brognola shared his evaluation of Pedro Ortiz with De Leo.

"Getting sent off to North Dakota or Ohio isn't going to be easy for these kids," she said with concern.

"Under the circumstances," Brognola said, "we have no choice. The boys have to be moved deeper underground. This location isn't secure. I'll make the arrangements for a private flight out this afternoon."

As he took the kitchen telephone from its wall mount, he added, "You'd better start getting their things together."

VISIBLY FRAZZLED, Conchita Balderas half walked, half ran down the winding street, toward the bus stop. Around the bend, well out of sight of the safehouse, was a dark blue Mercedes sedan. As she rushed up, a Mexican man in a gray three-piece suit got out on the passenger side and opened the rear door for her.

Balderas piled in the back with her bulky straw purse. Her cheeks were flushed, she was perspiring and she looked scared.

She had every reason to be.

For many years, Balderas had worked as a cook and maid at the safehouse, ever since it had been confiscated by the government in a big tax fraud case. Her Justice Department employers had always treated her fairly. She had never been given any reason to complain, and certainly never any reason to betray their trust.

Until now.

The Samosa cartel was offering an enormous sum of money for information about the location of the sons of Yovana Ortiz. Too much money for her to walk away from. She was too street-smart to try to make the deal herself. Instead, she took her information to her cousin, a lawyer in Tijuana. Balderas knew she had to protect her back or she would never see a dime of the reward. She correctly reasoned that a fifty-fifty split with Fidelio was much better than nothing.

Her cousin had organized the secure transfer of the reward money south of the border, where the U.S. government wouldn't find out about it. After consultation with Fidelio, Balderas had decided to keep her job for a while. Maybe even as long as a year, before quitting and returning to live in Mexico. If she followed the plan, nobody would ever be the wiser.

She did have a doctor's appointment this afternoon and she planned to keep it. She had expressed much concern to Agent De Leo about a lump that had appeared in the side of her neck. Her doctor had already assured her that it was nothing, a benign fatty tumor, but she had made a big deal out of it to De Leo to give herself an excuse to be someplace else, and to cover her nervousness over what was going to happen at the safehouse after she left.

When the car peeled away from the curb, the acceleration pushed Balderas deep into the leather seat. She became even more afraid and clutched her big purse tight to her bosom. The two men in the front of the Mercedes were large, with long, greasy black hair, and they smelled strongly of cologne. She didn't know either of them by name, but she was certain that they both worked for the Murillo brothers.

The man in the passenger's seat turned to speak to her. "If everything isn't exactly as you said, we'll find you," he told her. From under his suit jacket he took out a nickel-plated Beretta pistol with mother-of-pearl grips. Leaning between the front bucket seats, he pointed the gun at her heart. "We'll find you the same way we found the two boys, and you'll die."

"Only we'll cut you first," the driver promised over his shoulder. "Maybe burn you, too. And other things, even less pleasant...."

Balderas closed her eyes and swallowed hard. "Everything is as I described," she said. "I wouldn't lie to you."

"If you try to change your mind," the passenger said, "if you warn the Feds in the house about what is coming, you won't get your money, and you will die."

The Mercedes swerved over to the curb at the next bus stop. The passenger jumped out and opened the door for her.

"Don't forget," he warned as she stepped onto the sidewalk. "We can always find you."

With tires squealing, the car sped away.

Weak in the knees, Balderas sat on the bus stop bench. Her lower lip started to quiver and her eyes brimmed over with tears. Digging a wad of pink tissue from her purse, she began to sob brokenly into it. She knew terrible things were going to happen at the house, that the agents wouldn't give up the children without a fight, that good people were going to be shot and killed. Balderas felt terrible guilt about her part in that. But it was too late to do anything about it, now.

She had her own family to worry about, her own children and their children. America was about surviving, about making the best of one's opportunities.

Balderas prayed that whatever happened in the house, the sweet little boys would be safe from harm. As the city bus appeared down the street, she crossed herself and quickly stood, waving the wet pink tissue at the driver so he would stop.

Life had to go on.

SPECIAL AGENT Tom Fitzpatrick leaned on the railing of the safehouse's second-story balcony, scanning the far side of the canyon with a pair of high-powered binoculars. Trying to spot unnatural and potentially threatening movement was tough duty. From Fitzpatrick's vantage point, he could see all the way to the canyon floor, but it was even harder to tell what was going on down there. The bottom of the canyon was cut by a seasonal stream, now dry, and the streambed was overgrown, canopied with brush, spindly tree limbs and big branches that had fallen off the eucalyptus trees.

Because the job was largely impossible, Fitzpatrick was having trouble keeping his attention focused. He did his best to follow the established protocol, sweeping his field of view through the same, deliberate arc; an arc calculated to catch human movement, enemy approach along the bottom and up both sides of the canyon.

Agent Fitzpatrick didn't think the enemy, if they were coming, would make a rush from the canyon side. Such a move was strategically stupid, in his opinion. Unless it was part of a pincer attack, with a simultaneous assault from the street, the two boys and the agents protecting them would simply be pushed out of the front of the house into the neighborhood, where they could escape. He wasn't too concerned about an attack from the canyon, period. Busting brush wasn't the Murillos' style. They were more into urban warfare, car bombs, machine gun roadblocks, the massacre of unarmed civilians.

Fitzpatrick lowered the heavy binoculars and let them hang on the strap around his neck. He rubbed his eyes with his fingertips.

He didn't see the camouflage tape–wrapped muzzle of the .308 Winchester long gun poke out through the nasturtium leaves at the edge of the clearing, and he didn't see the man in a Ghillie suit with green war paint on his face whose hands were holding it.

OUTSIDE THE SAFEHOUSE, three federal agents sat in a parked van on the opposite side of the street. The man in the driver's seat was trying to listen to a baseball game on the van's radio, but it wasn't easy with the annoying drone of a pair of leaf-blowers working full blast a few doors down. The other two agents were in the back compartment, hidden from street view behind a thick curtain. They sat in front of a bank of built-in TV screens, drinking cold sodas. They were monitoring the output of a series of remote surveillance cameras attached to telephone poles up and down the block.

All three of the agents were heavily armed. They carried 9 mm H&K submachine guns, and .40-caliber SIG-Sauer handguns.

"Man," one of the men in back exclaimed, "I've seen some slow-moving gardeners before, but those guys take the cake."

For his partner's benefit, he pointed at the video image

of two Hispanic men working out of a Dodge pickup truck parked on the other side of the street. They were wearing Chargers baseball hats, big ear protectors and bandannas tied over their noses and mouths. The latter was to protect them from the flying grass and dust they were raising with their leaf-blowers. The gardeners kept going over and over the same area of sidewalk, like they were trying to polish it.

As the agents watched, the two gardeners shut off their leaf-blowers and headed back to their pickup at a crawl. They put the blowers into the bed, out of sight.

"We've got company," the agent in the driver's seat said. "Coming in fast."

A full-size moving van had turned the corner and was heading toward them. There was barely room for it to pass. The cars parked on both sides of the street made it so narrow that it was, in effect, one-way.

One of the agents in back jabbed his finger at the monitor with one hand, grabbing for his SMG with the other. "The gardeners, oh, Christ!"

The two gardeners had pulled M-16s from the truck bed. They immediately opened fire from across the street, shooting from the hip, stitching the side of the surveillance van with 5.56 mm lead.

There was no time to warn the safehouse.

No time to do anything.

The rear of the van rattled from dozens of hits, the video monitors exploded. The agents trapped in the back compartment were blown out of their chairs. They died without returning fire.

The agent in the driver's seat tried to bring his SIG to bear on the shooters, but before he could squeeze off a round, the van's windshield shattered inward. The shotgun blast from the front of the moving van slammed him back into his seat. He bounced forward, hit the dashboard and slumped across the console.

His face and neck had been ripped by double buckshot and jagged bits of glass. He choked on the blood pouring into his throat.

Someone opened the van's passenger door.

He caught the sound of a hammer locking back.

It was the last thing he heard.

WHEN THE GUNFIRE erupted from the street, Brognola was back on the patio, watching the boys jump into the spa. At almost the same instant, from the other side of the steel fence came the hard *crack* of a heavy-caliber rifle shot. Followed by the resounding smack of lead against flesh.

As Brognola's hand dipped inside his jacket for the butt of his SIG-Sauer P-229, he caught a blur of motion from the second story of the safehouse. Struck in the stomach by a sniper's bullet, Agent Fitzpatrick toppled over the balcony rail, did a slow somersault and crashed limply into a row of potted rose trees.

The Justice agent closest to the Jacuzzi lunged across the deck, jumping between the children and the fence, blocking them from fire with his own body. Before he could draw his weapon another rifle shot rang out. He clutched the middle of his chest, twisted and fell sideways into the hot tub.

Pedro and Juanito stood frozen in the tub, their arms stiff at their sides as they watched clouds of the dying man's blood turn the water red. Brognola rushed over to them, grabbed their arms and pulled them out of the hot tub. Pushing them flat to the deck, he swung up the .40-caliber pistol.

A shape moved on the other side of the fence.

He fired as fast as he could pull the trigger. The string of shots sparked off the steel bars. The shape fell away. And he heard a thump as the body hit the ground, then rolled downslope, back into the bush.

Agent De Leo rushed out of the French doors with her automatic pistol drawn.

As Brognola angled closer to the fence, peering over the sights of his weapon, he shouted to the boys, "Get back in the house!"

They jumped up and ran to De Leo, who pulled them inside.

Over his shoulder, Brognola heard the sounds of a battering ram breaking down the safehouse's front doors.

"They're coming in, sir!" De Leo said.

"Call in backup!" Brognola told her.

His words were smothered by the near-simultaneous racking booms of several short-barreled shotguns from inside the house, booms mixed with sustained bursts of full-auto gunfire.

Looking down the canyon, Brognola saw four men in sniper camouflage charging up the cleared section of slope. He took a double-handed grip on the SIG and fired three quick shots, hitting what he'd aimed at. The man on the far right crumpled facedown onto the grass. Before Brognola could retreat, fire from the other snipers blistered the fence, forcing him to dive to the deck.

Inside the house, a full-out firefight was raging. It was so intense that De Leo had been forced to move the boys back to the relative safety of the patio doorway. She hunkered over them there like a mother wolf. A mother wolf with a blue-steel SIG-Sauer.

"We've got three coming up the hill," Brognola shouted at her. As he spoke, more bullets clipped the fence above his head. He stuck his pistol over the top of the fence's brick base and without aiming fired back.

From the opposite direction inside the house, a hail of bullets crashed through the French doors, ricocheting across the flagstones, sending broken glass flying. Returning fire over her shoulder, back into the house, De Leo shoved the boys out onto the patio ahead of her. Another burst of autofire ripped through the doors. The female agent moaned and, grabbing her right leg, pitched forward onto the deck.

In three strides Brognola was at her side. She'd taken a hit in the right thigh. It looked serious.

"Can you walk?" he said.

Her face drained by shock and contorted with pain, Agent De Leo shook her head.

"Let's get you in the cabana with the boys," Brognola told her as he bent to help her up. "After I lure the snipers into the house, you can slip past them and get away down the canyon."

"I'm not going anywhere, sir," she said through tightly clenched teeth. "I think my leg's broken."

Brognola had feared as much from the location and entry angle of her leg wound. The slug had cracked, if not shattered, her thighbone.

"Either you hide with the kids and help them escape," De Leo said flatly, "or we're going to lose them. All this will have been for nothing."

The big Fed knew she was right. There was no time for hand-wringing or heartfelt condolences. The safehouse would be overrun by attackers in a few moments. If their positions had been reversed, Brognola the one who was wounded and De Leo still fully functional, he would have been the one to make the ultimate sacrifice and remain behind. Fate had made the choice for them.

This agent had proved herself more than worthy of Brognola's admiration and confidence, and his deepest respect.

"Go on, boys," he said, firmly pushing Pedro and Juanito toward the cabana. Then Brognola turned and looked back. He watched as Agent Madeline De Leo dragged herself over the threshold, back into the teeth of the firefight.

Seconds later, crouched behind the door of the cramped little room, Brognola sensed that the boys were still holding their breath, hoping against hope that this attack was a rescue attempt sponsored by their father. If he let them go on thinking that way, they might take the opportunity to cry out for help at exactly the wrong moment.

"We don't know who the people outside are," he told them. "They may have been sent here to kill you. You have to be very quiet and very still if any of us are going to get out of this alive."

MOANING FROM the blinding pain in her thigh and hip, Agent De Leo hauled herself on her belly, hand over hand, back into the house. Automatic weapon fire chattered from the floor above her. It was followed by the blast of a single shotgun and then a flurry of handgun fire. It appeared that the bad guys had already cleaned out the house's lower floor and with massed fire had driven the last of the federal agents to retreat up the stairs. Now the attackers were in the process of working them into an escapeproof corner. The upper story had a long hallway that connected to a master bedroom. From there, no further retreat was possible, except by jumping from the second-story balcony, which opened onto a fifty-foot drop into the canyon. De Leo had no doubt that the agents would be making their last stand in the big bedroom.

As quickly as she could, shutting out the pain and the fear she felt, De Leo dragged herself through the house. In the hallway, she came upon the body of one of her Justice team members. She didn't bother checking him for a pulse. He had been shot at least a dozen times at close range.

Behind her, over the sounds of shooting, she could hear boots crunching on broken glass. The snipers had entered the building from the patio. She had to hurry. De Leo grabbed the dead man's shotgun and his side arm and crawled on, pulling herself through a slurry of his mingled blood and guts.

When she reached the sunken living room, she let herself slide down the three steps to the carpet. Even though she turned onto her good side to do this, the successive bumps as she dropped down each stair jarred her wound. The surges of agony almost made her black out.

Overhead, the gun battle raged on. De Leo rolled to her back, a .40-caliber automatic pistol in each hand. She released both safeties and braced herself, elbows resting on the rug.

When the attackers charged down the hall above her, it sounded like a herd of elephants. She could see them coming, too. A curse on her lips, De Leo opened fire, shooting up through the ceiling as fast as she could pull the twin triggers. The blazing SIGs cut a ragged double line of bullet holes through the barrel-vaulted stucco. Smoking shell casings smacked her in the face, plaster dust rained on her. She squinted and kept shooting.

There were at least two heavy thuds as bodies hit the

floor above her. She let up on the triggers. The trample of feet on the hallway had stopped.

Zeroing in on the spots where the bad guys had gone down hard, De Leo emptied another ten shots into the ceiling. When the slides locked back, she tossed the handguns aside, grabbed the Ithaca shotgun and pulled herself behind a couch.

Suddenly it was very quiet in the house.

Quiet enough for her to hear a hushed back-and-forth in Spanish from an adjoining room.

The snipers.

Agent De Leo knew her position was worse than weak. She couldn't fire a scattergun kill-shot without popping out from above the back of the sofa, or from around the padded arms at either end. Jumping from behind cover was impossible due to her broken leg.

The end was close enough to taste.

Madeline De Leo was certain that she was going to die. That knowledge and an overwhelming desire to make her killers pay gave her a freedom of action that she otherwise would have lacked. If survival wasn't on the table, there were any number of ways for her take her pound of flesh.

She pressed her cheek to the carpet behind the couch. Its legs held it far enough off the ground so that, looking under it, she could see maybe three feet in front of it. De Leo cracked the pump slide back far enough to see the red plastic of the buckshot round already chambered. She thrust the stubby shotgun under the couch and held it there, finger on the trigger, waiting for her opportunity.

The gunfire resumed with a vengeance upstairs, hiding the sound of the approaching snipers. From under the couch she could see splats hitting the carpet. Splats of red. Blood was steadily dripping from the holes she'd shot in the ceiling.

De Leo held her breath. A pair of camouflage boots appeared on the other side of the couch.

The 20-gauge boomed from under the couch, sending a tongue of flame licking out over the carpet. As buckshot struck it point-blank, the sniper's right foot exploded. Bone and flesh scattered in all directions.

The sniper collapsed with a shriek, clutching his freshly made stump, trying to stop the high-spurting arterial blood with his hands. He screamed for help as he rolled on the rug in front of the couch.

De Leo pulled back the Ithaca and cycled the pump slide. This time the sniper saw the muzzle under the sofa.

It was pointed right at his forehead.

The shotgun roared, kicking back hard. De Leo didn't wait around to see the effect of the blast. Jerking the shotgun out from under the couch, she started crawling.

Full-automatic fire shook the sofa from end to end.

De Leo couldn't crawl fast enough to escape. She gasped as red-hot lances pierced her back and shoulder, skewering her to the floor.

The autofire from the other side of the living room stopped; upstairs it continued. As tufts of couch stuffing drifted down, she heard the snipers talking in Spanish. They had to speak loud to make themselves understood.

"Did we get him?"

"I can't see from here."

One more, she promised herself, cycling the shotgun's action. She could take out one more.

With the last of her strength, De Leo dragged herself to the wall that faced the back of the couch. She drew herself up, propping her shoulders and upper back against the wall. She held the stubby pump gun braced on her good knee.

The snipers would have to come around the ends of the couch to get her. They would have to expose themselves. She prepared herself for a split second reaction to movement.

When a head appeared on her right, she pivoted the Ithaca and fired. The shotgun leapt up from her knee, its muzzle bouncing off the wall beside her head. The face vanished in a puff of red, its flesh melted away by buckshot, and its bone turned to splinters that wetly pelted the four walls.

Grinning with fierce satisfaction, Agent De Leo turned to meet her destiny, a man dressed in a mesh-net sniper suit standing at the other end of the couch.

Without a word, the Mexican emptied his autorifle into her chest.

HAL BROGNOLA WATCHED the shadows pass on the other side of the cabana's gauzy curtains. When they were gone, he opened the door a crack. "Quick," he hissed at the boys as he ushered them out onto the patio. He pointed to the gate in the back fence. "That way," he said.

Pedro and Juanito jumped down from the gate to the grass of the cleared area at the top of the canyon's rim. As Brognola followed them, somebody shouted at him from the second-story balcony.

"Go!" he said to the boys, driving them ahead of him down the slope toward the wall of vegetation.

A volley of gunfire from the upper floor of the safehouse screamed over their heads, sailing into the branches and trunks of the eucalyptus forest.

"Keep running!" he shouted at the boys. "Don't stop! Whatever you do, don't stop!"

With Pedro and Juanito in the lead, they burst headlong into the dense scrub. In a matter of a dozen steps the going became alarmingly more steep. The waist-high plants were slick and their viny stems tripped the feet. Brognola fell hard, scrambled up and immediately fell again.

High above them, the shooting from the safehouse suddenly stopped. Which meant that all of the agents were either dead or otherwise taken out of action.

Brognola ignored his pain and hurled himself down the slope. Through a gap in the branches and tree trunks of eucalyptus below, he could see the bottom of the canyon.

To the right, the dried-up streambed tracked uphill to the top of the mesa. To the left, it wound down the canyon to the mouth where it met a frontage road that bordered Highway 8. Big hotels lined that road. Hotels with people, cover, law enforcement. It was their only chance.

Unable to stop their descent, Brognola and the two boys crashed through the screen of manzanita and onto the stream's gravel. Above and behind them, they heard the sounds of men breaking through the trees.

"That way!" Brognola said, pointing to the left.

Being shorter and more agile than Brognola, not to mention younger, the boys had an easier time getting under the maze of overhanging branches. Brognola had to work hard to keep up with them. In some places, this meant climbing over fallen eucalyptus trees. Pepper trees and wild olives grew right in the middle of the streambed, forcing him to claw his way through the tangled cascade of limbs.

The sound of the freeway was louder. They were getting close to the frontage road. "Keep going!" he urged the boys. Sweat poured off him, soaking his ripped suit jacket and dirt-stained pants.

Behind them, he could hear boots crunching on gravel. The pursuit was gaining.

The big Fed didn't reach for his holstered pistol. This wasn't the time for a standoff. Not when they were outnumbered, outgunned and caught in dense, brushy cover.

The stream channel curved to the right, ending in a massive, concrete culvert. The boys skidded to a stop.

"Over the top!" Brognola shouted at them. He scrambled up the incline after the boys. They raced down a dirt path that opened onto the back side of a five-story motor hotel, a multilevel parking garage and a wide asphalt parking lot.

At the far end of the building, a security guard stood at his post in front of the entrance. He was looking the other way. The few hotel guests in the parking lot were busy getting their luggage into or out of their car trunks.

"Run!" Brognola ordered the boys. They were less than one hundred yards from safety.

As he shouted, a dark-green minivan with a black windows shot into the parking lot. It screeched to a stop in front of them, blocking their path and the security guard's view of the action. The side door slid open, and a pair of Mexican men with heavy-caliber automatics hopped out.

Brognola started to go for his SIG, but thought better of it. The Mexicans had the drop on him. One of them disarmed him, then the other stepped up and punched him full in the face.

The blow staggered Brognola but he kept his feet. The

big Fed turned his head aside and spit blood onto the asphalt.

A second or two later, the men pursuing them appeared at the trailhead. They pulled the boys into the back of the van with them, leaving Brognola outside.

One of the Mexicans holding a handgun on him said, "What should we do with him? I say we shoot him, here."

"No," said a voice from the van's front passenger seat, "this one has things to tell us." The black-tinted power window whirred softly as it dropped out of sight into the passenger door.

Brognola stared into a face he recognized—the face of Ramon "Three Nails" Murillo.

12

The rear wall of Dr. Hector Perpuly's private office was covered with framed official-looking diplomas from distinguished institutions around the world. A few of these documents were real, but most were mere decoration, bought by mail order from a printer in Des Moines, Iowa. The wall of honors was intended to put his clients at ease with his professional training and experience.

None of the doctor's potential patients had ever bothered to walk up and examine the documents closely. If they had, and if they could have deciphered the ornate calligraphy, they might have noticed strange variations on standard spellings—Slone/Ketering, Meyo Clinic, Solk Institute.

With one of Don Jorge Samosa's pet Colombians leaning across his desk, breathing mint Binaca in his face, with three more Shining Path thugs blocking the only exit door behind him, the doctor was thinking less of art than of his own skin. The room seemed claustrophobic, airless; his situation suddenly desperate.

Many times in the past the doctor had performed various procedures for members of the Samosa cartel. Although he'd come in contact with drug criminals before, the Colombians were in a league of their own when it came to animalistic brutality.

Looming over the desk, Enrique Tomás was saying that while Perpuly was renowned for his skill with the tummy tuck, the Colombian specialty was something even more readily apparent. Tomás had then gone on to describe this "specialty" in detail. First, he'd said the individual's throat was slashed from ear to ear. Then, the slasher would reach into the open wound with bare fingers, grip the tongue by the base and pull the whole thing down through the gaping slit. To illustrate the result, Tomás had then gleefully flapped his necktie in Perpuly's face.

The other Colombians had found this most amusing.

Perpuly had to pretend to smile and chuckle for fear of offending these animals. They had come on a mission for the drug lord Samosa, a mission that in the doctor's professional judgment was ill-advised.

"Medically speaking," Perpuly said, "moving the patient at this time isn't a prudent thing to do. He has suffered severe facial and leg injuries and there is already some infection, which needs to be closely monitored if it is to be kept under control. His prognosis would be better if he remained in the clinic for another three or four days, at least."

"If he doesn't come with us," Tomás said, "I guarantee you that his prognosis is going to be fatal almost immediately."

"Well, in that case, there is nothing more to be discussed," Perpuly said, pushing up from behind his desk. "The patient is of course free to go at any time he wishes."

With that, the plastic surgeon dismissed any and all responsibility in the matter. The last thing he wanted was to have to explain to the San José police how a patient recuperating under his care happened to accidentally receive a Colombian necktie job.

ENRIQUE TOMÁS leaned over the stainless-steel rails of the hospital bed, peering closely at the half-bandaged face of the sleeping patient. Roberto *"El Azote"* Murillo lay on his back, his one visible eye closed, his mouth hanging open below the wad of gauze and adhesive tape, snoring loudly. Clear drip lines of intravenous fluids, antibiotics, sedatives and painkillers were connected to both arms.

Grinning at his men, Tomás took a seven-inch silver-pommeled stiletto from a belt sheath inside his jacket. With the pointed tip of the narrow blade, he carefully lifted the edge of the bloody bandage, trying to get a look at what lay underneath. He was very curious, as were the others, about just how messed up Murillo's face was. With the knife's razor edge he carefully slit the strips of tape that held the compress. This done, he used the blade to flip the gauze out of the way.

"Looks like a baboon's butt, all red and purple and swollen," one of the men behind him said.

"Look at all those stitches," another thug said.

Tomás did better than that. He slipped the tip of the stiletto under one of the black loops of thread and, with a quick flick of the wrist, cut it.

"Ow!" Murillo exclaimed as he jolted awake, grabbing defensively for his face.

Tomás drew back the knife, but slowly.

Roberto Murillo pulled the bandage back over his wounds and held it to the side of his face.

Tomás could see the alarm in Murillo's bloodshot eye.

It pleased him. It pleased him to have the man strung up like a turkey, without weapons or bodyguards.

The Colombian knew he could fuck with him more, if he wanted to.

And he wanted to.

"You sleep too much, Roberto," he said. "You Mexicans are so lazy. Always need your siesta."

"What do you want?" Murillo said thickly, despite his discomfort, struggling to a sitting position. The bodyguards Ramon had left outside his hospital room were gone. The Colombians circled his bed like vultures. Vultures in thousand-dollar suits.

"The noise didn't wake you, then?" Tomás asked.

"What noise?"

"You could hear it all over town. It broke windows a mile away."

"I don't know what you're talking about." Murillo reached for a glass of water on his bedside table and drank, swallowing hard.

"In that case, there's something on the television that you should see." Tomas picked up the remote and turned on the set, which hung on a bracket on the opposite wall. He switched channels until he got the one that he was looking for.

The screen showed a picture of a burning building surrounded by fire trucks. Firemen directed towering streams of water onto the flaming ruin. Droves of police cars were parked back from the fire. Uniformed officers strung the perimeter with yellow tape. In the foreground, one of the cops was holding up the corner of a blue plastic sheet to get a peek of the body that lay beneath it on the ground.

"Do you recognize it?" Tomás said.

To Murillo, the burning building looked like it had been hit by a bomb. "Should I?" he replied.

"It's where the Lord of the Seas keeps his gold."

Murillo squinted to see more clearly, grimacing at the twinge of pain that particular muscle movement caused him. On closer inspection, he realized he knew the place.

"Stop that!" Murillo said to the Colombians standing to the right of his bedside. Two of the Shining Path animals were amusing themselves by playing around with his intravenous lines, pinching them off, fiddling with the drip-rate controls and with the control panel of his electronic monitor. They looked at him like he was a bug.

"They really fucked up the depository," Tomás said. "Whoever they were, they also fucked up the men inside guarding it. Sounds kind of familiar, doesn't it?"

Murillo stared at the TV screen. The picture had changed. It turned out that the earlier shot was videotaped. In real time, a live camera showed fire rescue crews pulling a handful of dirty, battered men from a side window. Survivors trapped in the rubble.

"Did they get the gold?" Murillo asked.

"They didn't even try," Tomás told him. "It wasn't part of the plan."

"I don't understand."

The Colombian gave Murillo an incredulous look. "It's simple. Whoever attacked the depository didn't care about taking the gold for themselves. They just wanted Don Jorge to not have access to it anymore."

Murillo frowned and reached for his water glass again.

"The government will confiscate the gold as illegal drug profits or nonpayment of taxes, or something," Tomás said. "Samosa can kiss it all goodbye. He isn't happy."

But Tomás was; Murillo could see that. The reason why was about to become evident.

"Don Jorge hopes you are feeling better and wants to talk to you in person," Tomás said.

"As soon as I'm released, of course."

"You are released."

At a signal from Tomás, a pair of nurses come into the room and started unhooking Murillo from monitor and drip lines.

"Why does he want to talk to me?" Murillo asked.

With a wry expression on his face the Colombian said, "You've got to be kidding."

"Why me?" Murillo repeated.

"Because unfortunate things have happened. And now more bad things. He needs for you to explain certain coincidences."

"I was here in the clinic," Murillo protested. "I was heavily sedated. How could I have had anything to do with what happened across town?"

"That's what I told Samosa myself. I said these two Mexicans couldn't possibly have done this thing. The attack was too well planned and too well executed. They would have found a way to fuck it up somehow. I think he agreed with me."

"My brother..."

"Assuming Ramon hasn't screwed up the mission in the States, he'll be coming down to meet with Don Jorge in person, too. If he messed it up, he's already dead."

The nurses hustled an unresisting Murillo out of the bed. With ruthless efficiency, they dressed him in the clothes he had been brought in with. Clothes still spattered with dried blood. Then they made him sit in a wheelchair. Murillo looked and felt like hell, his bandages half hanging off, his face bloated and swollen.

Dr. Perpuly appeared in the doorway. He didn't protest what was happening to his patient. He knew who was in control here, and it wasn't him. As one of the nurses wheeled Murillo from the room, Perpuly placed a paper bag full of pill bottles in his lap.

"Take these antibiotics every four hours," he said. "Have someone change your dressing every day. Try to keep it clean. You'll be fine."

The expression in the doctor's eyes told Murillo he didn't believe a word he'd just said.

13

Pacific Coast, Panama-Costa Rica border, 7:52 p.m.

Mack Bolan watched the forty-seven-foot ketch powering without sails a thousand yards to the north, already well across the border into Costa Rica. The ship glowed like it was on fire, from stem to stern, from crow's nest to waterline. It glided over a glassy, vermillion sea.

If the sailboat was elegant, the vessel tracking it was anything but. Bolan's transportation was a long-liner scow. The twenty-eight-foot wooden powerboat had low freeboard and a narrow beam. Its wheelhouse superstructure was made of weathered sheet plywood. Square holes had been cut in it to make windows. The cramped rear deck was stacked with longline floats: black pennants made of strips of garbage bags tied on the ends of long, slender wooden poles. The superstructure had been painted white, a long time ago. A propane tank was lashed to the bow platform with bungee cords, partially blocking the view out the port-side window. As it chugged along, clouds of black, gritty exhaust spewed from twin ports in the stern.

This seagoing wreck, this diesel-powered shanty had no official name. Its skipper, an expatriate American, ex-Special Ops named Vorhees, affectionately called it *"The Shit Bucket."*

Bolan glanced back at the makeshift chart table behind him. For a pile of junk, the long-liner was equipped with some serious state-of-the-art computer gear. And not just the usual satellite-link navigational hardware. On one of the LCD screens was a complete architect's blueprint of the vessel they were pursuing. Stony Man Farm had provided the intel. The ketch was a Wittholz, all aluminum, built in 1982. It had a center cockpit, and fore and aft access to its below-deck salons.

"Drug runner's slowing down," the skipper announced.

Vorhees had gone native. His skin had been roasted the color of coffee. He wore only a pair of filthy cutoff jeans. There were work scars on his feet, shins and hands. His baseball cap was decorated with a combination of marine grease, sweat, fish guts and bird shit. Downwind, he smelled like stale Imperial beer.

From overhead came a loud thumping noise. The long-liner's one-and-only mate, who was standing watch on top of the wheelhouse, was stamping his bare feet. Then Virgilio's wide face appeared upside down through the front window. He was smiling.

"Looks like our friends are calling it a night," Vorhees said.

Through the front porthole Bolan saw the big sailboat coming about. Having passed the reefs at Punta Burica, they were looking for a spot to throw out the hook.

"What say we backtrack our course a little?" Vorhees suggested. "We don't want to crowd these turkeys too close, make them think we're too interested."

"Yeah," Bolan agreed. "Let's put some distance between us."

The scow did a slow 180-degree turn. As it did, the rattle of the sailboat's anchor chain drifted across the water. Off the stern, the Executioner watched the mast-top anchor light wink on. The ketch lay in a small bay just off the beach, protected from the westerly swell by the reef and the skinny finger of the Burica peninsula. Bobbing in the wake of the long-liner was something that looked like a log. It was, in fact, Virgilio's dugout canoe tethered to the scow with a towline.

Vorhees motored south, back toward Panama. The border between the two countries, once disputed, had been recently turned into a jointly operated national park. Neither country had a standing army anymore, which meant they could both spend more money on ed-ucation and health services for their people. It also meant that most of the coastline in this area was unguarded and unobserved.

According to intel, the Samosa cartel was taking full advantage of the peace.

Vorhees steered along the edge of the peninsula. Palm trees ran a sparse line down its spine. It ended in a spit of land that jutted out into the Pacific. Because of the hazardous reef, Vorhees gave the tip of the spit a wide berth.

After motoring around the far side of the peninsula, he brought the scow in close to shore, killed the engine and coasted to a stop. They were about forty yards from the sandy beach.

"This should be close enough," he said.

Virgilio jumped down to the foredeck and hurried to drop the anchor off the bow.

"Seems like Miller time to me," the skipper said. He opened the red-and-white Igloo cooler at his feet, next to the helm. "Beer?" He offered Bolan a dripping brown bottle of Imperial.

The soldier waved it off. "I've got too much to do," he said. "Don't want to be slowed down."

"Gotcha," Vorhees said. He put the edge of the bottlecap on the metal trim of the dash and gave it a precise whack with the heel of his hand. Foam gushed out the neck.

But not for long.

Bolan watched the man drink half the bottle in a single gulp. Vorhees wiped his mouth with the back of his hand.

"Damn, that's good!" he said. "Why don't we go sit out on the veranda while Virigilo cooks up our supper? Virgilio, supper, please."

The *indio* nodded agreeably from the bow.

Bolan and the skipper stepped out of the open rear of the wheelhouse and moved aft. They took seats in a pair of folding lawn chairs. Vorhees put the cooler on the deck between them, then propped his bare feet on the stern.

"Been watching these suspect drug boats for better than a year," Vorhees said. "I've got to tell you, working undercover for the DEA sure beats the hell out of fishing for a living. I do my snooping, I make my reports, I get my money paid in nice big chunks."

"So, there's no actual interdiction in these waters?"

"Hey, the police run around in dinky skiffs. Look at them sideways and they swamp."

"If it's never been searched, how do you know that the Wittholz over there is part of the smuggling operation?"

Vorhees quickly finished his beer and started a second. "It's only logical if you look at the big picture," he said. "We've got a series of big oceangoing pleasure boats anchoring at night off a river mouth, about fifty miles north of here. Little boats come down the river at night, and stuff is off-loaded and on-loaded. The little boats zoom back up the river. Our drug runner has parked there many times before, but he's never tried it in the dark. The anchorage there is kind of tricky. There are some nasty reefs along the shoreline, and the swell can put you aground in a hurry. Way it looks, the skipper ain't up to it. He'd rather wait until tomorrow.''

"What's happening with the small boats? You said cargoes were being taken off as well as loaded."

"No way to be sure. Some ships arrive full and leave empty. The cartel might be doing it to confuse the Coast Guard patrols up north. They stop boats that have stopped here and come up with nothing. Could be the cartel is putting together specific shipments for specific buyers. Storing the goods up in the jungle until the pickup vessel arrives."

"I've seen the satellite recon of that section of the Osa peninsula."

Vorhees smirked. "Not much to see, is there? Rain forest canopy in the national park is too damned thick. Nice spot to do something illegal."

"Have you been in there?"

"I got close one time," the skipper said. "One night, on a high tide, Virgilio and I snuck into the river mouth's estuary in his dugout canoe. We paddled a couple of miles up into the park." Vorhees pointed at two white scars on the top of his sun-browned foot. "See that?"

"Snake bite?" Bolan said.

"Yup. Goddamned *fer-de-lance*. Sucker was eight feet long, and all of it mean. We'd beached the dugout and had hiked about a half mile into the bush when it nailed me. Put its fang right through the top of my rubber boot. Came back to hit me again, but Virgilio whacked it with his machete. I was okay for about ten minutes, then the poison started to work. I was one sick puppy. Virgilio had to carry me the last fifty yards. It took me a month to recover, but that wasn't the worst of it.''

"Oh, yeah?''

"The poison did something bad to my spleen, permanent damage if you can believe the doctors in Golfito. One thing's for sure, though, I can't drink like I used to.''

Bolan didn't say anything.

"Yeah, if I do more than a six-pack at a time, my blood pressure drops to near nothing. Fucking snakes. The Osa's crawling with them. They hunt at night, you know. If you go in there, you'd better watch where you step and what's in the trees overhead. The snakes will jump down on you. We got snakes in the ocean, here, too. Nasty looking black-and-yellow things that will kill you in a minute. Only good thing about them is their fangs are way back in their jaws, so unless they get hold of something small, like a finger or your nose, even if they bite, they don't get any venom in you.''

"So you never actually saw the storage site?'' Bolan said.

"Nah. And you won't catch me going in there again for a second try. Not for a million bucks.''

Virgilio clanked a big iron skillet on the propane burner in the scow's wheelhouse.

As Vorhees opened his third beer with the back of a rusty sheath knife, he said, "Hope you're hungry. Virgilio fries a mean banana.''

UNDER A SKY choked with stars, Virgilio paddled the canoe up onto the shadowy beach. The Executioner stepped out of the bow into shin-deep water. It was warm. Maybe eighty-five degrees. He helped Virgilio slide the dugout higher onto the beach.

There was no moon, just stars. The palm trees at the edge of the jungle were silhouetted by them.

Bolan took his pack out of the canoe and followed the muscular little man up the beach toward Punta Burica. The landscape before them had no color. Sand, trees and water were all varying shades of gray, edging to black.

Approaching the treeline, Virgilio unsheathed his machete. "Stay close," he said softly over his shoulder.

Crossing the neck of the spit, they had to pass into the deep shadow of the palms. There was a lot of debris from the trees, fallen palm fronds, coconut hulls and flotsam washed up to the high tide mark. Bolan concentrated on the ground directly ahead of him, but the effort was wasted. It was so dark that it was impossible to tell what he was stepping on.

When they reached the other side of the point, the sailboat's anchor and cabin lights were visible up the beach. Virgilio's route led them along the forest's edge, in the deep shadow, where they had to walk to keep from being seen.

When they got within a hundred yards of the ketch, Virgilio stopped. He looked at Bolan and hooked a thumb at the boat.

The Executioner nodded. They were close enough.

Standing in the shadows of the palms, he put down his backpack and opened it. Taking out a pair of binoculars, Bolan scanned the vessel. The instrument lights were on in the central cockpit, but it was deserted. Much brighter lights were on in the main cabin aft. As he searched the illuminated portholes, he could hear the hum of the generator across the water. A man's head moved past his field of view. The forward cabin was dark, its occupants apparently already asleep.

Bolan handed the binoculars to Virgilio and took out his sound-suppressed Beretta 93-R. The pistol was sealed in a waterproof, clear-plastic case. He hooked the case to the nylon web belt around his waist, shifting the weight of the weapon to the small of his back. Also hanging from the belt was a SEAL-2000 sheath knife and a waterproof, gooseneched minispotlight.

Without a word, the Executioner kicked off his shoes, quickly crossed the open stretch of beach and slipped into the water.

He swam away from shore in quiet, powerful strokes, pausing every so often to check the position of the man on anchor watch, and make sure he hadn't come out on deck. As Bolan got closer to the hull, over the noise of the generator, he heard the sound of a television playing. He hadn't noticed it before, but there was a satellite dish on the main mast.

The Executioner made his way soundlessly to the ship's bow. He caught hold of the anchor chain and climbed it, hand over hand, up onto the bow pulpit. Ducking under the stainless-steel rails, he moved down the pulpit to the foredeck and crouched there. In a second, he had the Beretta out of its protective bag, safety off, ready to fire.

From the stern of the sailboat came a burst of laughter. Canned laughter from the television. Water was dripping off the hem of his swimming trunks, splattering on the deck. Keeping low, he moved to the cabin's front hatch and opened it a crack. In the glow of the anchor light above him, he could see six steps leading down. From inside the cabin, he heard a sound like a cat crying.

From the observations made earlier in the day, Bolan

knew that there were four people on the ship. Three men and a woman. According to Stony Man, none of them were the actual owners of the boat. One guy was a charter captain, the other three were deckhands and a cook. It was possible that the registered owners didn't know what these folks were up to. Having passed through the Panama Canal, it looked like the crew was either moving the boat to the west coast to pick up the owners or to return it to its permanent moorage. Under the name *Happy Landings* on the stern of the vessel was its home port: Seattle.

Bolan descended the steps partway, then reached back and closed the hatch behind him. He paused to let his eyes adjust to the dim light coming through the portholes.

This was the tough part.

He had to walk among the sleeping crew and verify that the boat was carrying drugs. He had to do it without waking anyone and without killing anyone, if possible. Otherwise, he might as well pack it in.

The front salon was empty. There were no signs of drugs. The strange cat sounds were getting louder.

Crossing the cabin, he turned the handle of the bulkhead door. As he knew from the vessel's schematics, it opened onto a narrow, windowless hallway that ended in another bulkhead. On both sides of the corridor were stateroom doors.

The persistent noise was coming from behind the one on his right. Bolan pushed on the handle and opened it a crack. The light through the open porthole shone on the single bunk, and the two people making love amid tangled sheets. The woman was making the cat sound.

The Executioner pulled the door closed.

He tried the next door on the left and found the stateroom empty. Stepping inside, he flicked on his minispotlight, playing it over the unmade bunk and bare walls. It looked like the skipper's quarters. A small bookcase held a library of nautical works, as well as porno paperbacks and skin mags. Bolan found the overhead light, pried open the housing with his sheath knife and unscrewed the lightbulb.

With his minispotlight, he located the bilge access indicated by the shipmaker's blueprint. The hinged deck plate was hidden under a rug beside the bunk. He opened the plate and aimed his light inside.

No bilge was visible.

Just an interlocking grid of white plastic parcels.

In order to stick his head inside and have a look around, he had to remove quite a few of the packages. He guessed there was probably a ton of cocaine hidden there.

Bolan had replaced the parcels and was closing the hatch when a door opened across the hallway. Bare feet padded past him, then came the thud of a balled fist pounding on a door closer to the stern. In a moment, two pairs of bare feet returned up the hall. One continued on to the cook's cabin, the other stopped at the captain's door.

The changing of the guard.

As the skipper's cabin door opened, the Executioner moved behind it, putting his back to the wall.

"Shit," the man said, as he tried the light switch. The captain stepped inside and shut the door behind him. He fumbled his way across the stateroom, then threw himself facedown on the bunk with a groan.

In the deep shadow, Bolan stood absolutely still, the Beretta raised in his hand, ready to fire.

It took three minutes for the guy to fall asleep.

Three minutes of dead calm on the Executioner's part, while he listened to his bathing suit drip on the deck, the creak of the vessel at anchor and the man's raspy breathing. When the breathing became slow and regular, and the guy was snoring, Bolan opened the hall door and looked out.

No one in sight.

Shutting the door behind him, he retraced his route back toward the bow. As he passed the cook's door, he noted that the cat sounds had resumed inside. New partner, same dance.

Bolan moved into the front salon. As he did so, through the portholes set high on the wall on the right side, in the glow of the anchor light, he caught movement. A man's hairy legs moved past the windows.

Apparently, the guy on watch was doing a walk-around.

The Executioner had known there was an additional risk of discovery if he swam to the boat. The question was, would the deckhand notice the wet footprints he had left behind? Would the crewman follow them from the bow pulpit to the forward hatch?

Bolan took a position beside the salon's daybed, bent onto one knee, with the Beretta's sights angled up at the top of the steps. In this case, the noise suppressor didn't guarantee a silent kill. Chances were, a fatal shot would mean that the man would collapse and fall from the stairs, hitting the deck with a thud so loud that it would rouse the others.

He wasn't worried about facing the rest of the sailboat's crew. Before they could get out of bed, Bolan would be off the boat, swimming for shore in the dark.

But if he was forced to show his hand there, the cartel

would be forewarned and the mission against the stronghold in the jungle would have to be scrubbed.

Keep walking, he thought as the crewman approached the bow.

The footsteps stopped directly in front of the hatch.

After a tense moment, the guy continued. Bolan could see his legs through the portholes as he rounded the deck on the other side of the salon.

The Executioner strained to hear the man's footsteps as he moved out of sight. All he could hear were cat sounds and rhythmic squeaking. He couldn't tell if the crewman was still on deck or not.

Bolan waited a minute or two, then climbed the steps and eased open the hatch.

For all he knew, the guy was lying in wait on top of the cabin's roof, with a weapon pointed toward the bow ready to ambush him. If he retreated, if he walked the length of the boat in order to jump off the stern, he had no guarantee that the guy wasn't back there watching TV. There was really no better choice than to go out the way he'd come.

The Executioner pushed forward through the hatch, pivoting to swing the Beretta's sights up at the roof.

Nobody there.

Crouching low to the deck, he moved to the corner of the cabin's superstructure and peered around it. The third guy was still on deck. He was flat on his belly, his head thrust partway through the porthole, trying to get a look at what was going on in the cook's cabin.

Bolan slipped the Beretta back in its waterproof bag and crossed the foredeck in two long strides. A second later, he was under the bow's rail, swinging onto the anchor line. He lowered himself into the water and, floating on his back, quietly kicked away shoreward from the hull. He wanted to make sure no one saw him depart.

Fifty yards away, he turned and stroked for the beach. Reaching the sand, he ran up to the shadows of the tree-line, then headed south.

"Psst," came a sound from the bush on his left.

Bolan stopped. As he turned, the SEAL-2000 knife came up in his hand, ready to strike.

Virgilio stepped out of the darkness. Starlight reflected off his broad, toothy grin.

"Is good?" he whispered as he handed Bolan back his shoes.

"Yeah, very good, my friend."

14

Punta Burica, 3:30 p.m.

The *Happy Landings* didn't pull up anchor first thing the next morning. Instead, it remained just off the beach.

As the day dragged on and the tropical sun drove the temperature past the mid-nineties, Vorhees became more and more impatient. The air hung dead still and heavy with humidity. Finally, the skipper couldn't take it any longer and started the engine. He ordered Virgilio to haul in the anchor.

"It'll be cooler offshore," he told Bolan as they chugged past the tip of the spit.

The Executioner nodded. The breeze created by the boat's movement had already made things more pleasant.

"Don't worry," Vorhees said, steering the long-liner seaward, "we'll keep the ragman in sight. Flat calm day like this, we'll be able to see the top of that main mast of his from ten miles out."

"We know where he's going to park it this night, anyway," Bolan said. "If you're going to drive around for a while, I'm going to hit the rack. Give me a shout when the sailboat pulls anchor."

He eased himself through the low, crudely cut doorway that led down into a cramped, cluttered cabin under the foredeck. The soldier crawled into one of the hammocks strung up there and fell into a heavy, dreamless sleep.

Virgilio awakened him about midafternoon. *"Señor,"* the mate said, "the other boat is moving."

The Executioner dismounted from the hammock and climbed into the wheelhouse. Vorhees was scanning the east with a huge pair of binoculars. He handed them to his passenger. "Go ahead, check it out," he said. "The drug runner is heading north, right on schedule."

Bolan climbed onto the foredeck, then on top of the wheelhouse roof. "He's got no canvas up," he called down to the bridge. "Still not sailing. Not enough wind running, I guess."

"Too much work in this heat, anyway," Vorhees said out the window. "At the rate he's chugging along, he'll probably make the river mouth a little before sunset."

As the scow changed course northward to parallel the ketch, Bolan returned to the wheelhouse and the wobbly chart table. He compared a topographic map of the Osa peninsula with a series of ten-hour-old satellite recon photos. Most of the Osa was Costa Rican national park, a huge, isolated area with hardly any human population. The river in question, the Rio Verde, had headwaters high in the protected rain forest. It snaked through sheer canyons and impenetrable jungle before it widened out near the coast. An estuary had formed at its mouth, blocked from the sea at low tide. On the satellite photos, some buildings were evident on the shore of the estuary.

Vorhees noticed what he was looking at and said, "Those little buildings on the north side of the lagoon are no-frills ecotourist lodges. No screens, no airconditioning. They cater to birders, mostly. The lodge owners keep their mouths shut about what's going on upriver. Ask them about the ruckus at night and they'll say it's from the gold mining, but that's just so much BS. If there's gold up there, my man, it's white and it's powdery.''

"What time's the high tide?"

"Not until close to midnight."

"Are we going to have trouble getting in through the breakers in that canoe?"

"It's nothing Virgilio can't handle. He was born in one of those dugouts. When the tide's most of the way up, things smooth out over the bar." Vorhees paused, then added, "One thing you've got to keep in mind if you do lose it is the bull sharks."

"You mean in the surf?"

"Yeah, there, too. They like to hunt in the cloudy water from the river runoff, maybe because they can sneak up on their prey without being seen. Come high tide, they swim right over the bar and into the river looking for treats. They're real dangerous in the river. They have no fear, they'll attack anything—cattle, horse, man. They swim inland to the limit of the tidal flow, maybe a mile from the beach, then follow the fall of the tide back out. You don't ever want to be wading in that river except on a dead low tide, when the bar is closed up at the mouth."

"These satellite infrared scans show evidence of some sort of encampment about two miles upriver, on the southern border of the park," Bolan said. "That would be the cartel storage area?"

"Like I said, I never made it up that far," Vorhees replied. "Nobody goes there. Or if they do, they don't come back. There've been reports of poachers and gold panners who've gone missing up the Rio Verde. The local police never poked their noses in to find out what happened to any of them. Christ, you should see those guys. Idiots with badges. A total joke. The national park rangers give the hot zone a wide berth, too. Not because of cartel bribes or basic incompetence, but because it's too dangerous. I've heard rumors about an army up there—mostly ex-Noriega paramilitaries—guarding the drug operation and killing trespassers on sight. There's been talk of booby-trapped game trails. There are no roads into the site, but there's a helicopter pad.

"Yeah, I see it on the photo," Bolan said. "Looks like there's just enough room for one chopper to land."

"We had a report from your people while you were sacking out," Vorhees said. "A helicopter slipped in and out at daybreak this morning. Touched down and then took off immediately. It probably dropped someone off or picked someone up. The helicopter flew on to Panama City."

"Based on the topo map, it looks like an upriver, underwater assault is out of the question."

"Yeah, the river's too shallow, only a couple of feet deep, and it runs too fast that high in the park. No way to get up it without power. That's why the cartel uses jet boats to run it. Your best bet is an overland approach. Virgilio is a good man. He'll get you there, safely. What you do once you're there is up to you. Smartest thing would be to turn right around and come back, but somehow I don't think you're going to do that. As the saying goes, it's your funeral."

"You can bet it's going to be somebody's funeral, anyway," Bolan said, as he dragged his black ballistic-nylon duffle bag from under the table into the middle of the wheelhouse floor. Unzipping it, he started pulling out his gear, getting ready for the night's mission.

He set aside the two pairs of night-vision goggles he'd

brought along, then drew out a padded, long-gun case. From the custom sheath he took a Steyr SSG P-IV urban sniper rifle, scoped with a Litton M-938 night-vision scope. The bolt gun was chambered for 7.62 mm NATO rounds. Intended for short-range sniper work, he figured its heavy-caliber bullet would have less of a tendency to deflect in dense cover. After checking the weapon, he resheathed it in the padded case.

Digging back into the duffle, Bolan produced a 9 mm Heckler & Koch submachine gun. Beside it on the deck, he set the Beretta 93-R and extra magazines for both. His combat harness was preloaded with frag and Thunderflash grenades. Then out came the body armor and finally, two more of the compact, high explosive satchel charges he'd used to level the Samosa gold depository in San José.

The deadweight of the entire lot had to be upward of ninety-five pounds.

"You plan to carry all that stuff through the bush?" Vorhees asked in disbelief.

"Virgilio can help me lug it partway up," the soldier said as he began to stow and rattleproof the gear into a pair of medium-size backpacks.

"Yeah, if it doesn't sink the dugout first," Vorhees said with a laugh.

The first mate was looking at the military hardware with more than keen interest.

"Man, you shouldn't have shown him all that shit," Vorhees said, shaking his head. "He loves firepower. You'll be wanting to pat down your new friend and inventory all of it before you leave."

"Very macho," Virgilio muttered as Bolan slipped the H&K into one of the packs.

ONE HOUR BEFORE the peak of the high tide, the stars were out in profusion once again. Through the night-vision binoculars Vorhees had on hand, some five hundred yards away Bolan saw a tiny fleet of jet-drive boats popping out of the estuary entrance, plowing through the lines of surf. He could hear them, too. At a distance of a half mile, they sounded like angry hornets.

Past the breakers, the jet boats motored up to the ketch, which had anchored just off the river mouth. Two of the boats took turns pulling up alongside the larger ship, while the other boats circled slowly, standing watch. With the aid of the night-vision binoculars, Bolan could see armed men in the bows of the patroling boats. After the white parcels were off-loaded onto the cargo boats, all the speed boats regrouped and zoomed in formation over the foaming bar and out of sight up the estuary.

Bolan lowered the binoculars and stepped back into the wheelhouse. It was darker than the pit of hell inside the long-liner scow. They were drifting without lights, engine silent, letting the current push them along the black, humid coastline.

"You two better get cracking," Vorhees said. "I don't want to drift too close to the drug runners."

Virgilio drew in the tow rope, pulling the dugout alongside the scow. He quickly stacked the two heavy backpacks amidship in the canoe. Bolan climbed in front, the *indio* took the stern.

"Watch out for the snakes," Vorhees cheerfully reminded them as they pushed off.

They began paddling south with the current. Virgilio steered them over the rise and fall of gentle surf, waves that ended in a roar along the narrow strip of beach left by the high tide. When they pushed off from the scow, they were about a quarter of a mile north of the river mouth. They moved at a brisk pace, aiming for the white masthead light of the sailboat.

The canoe passed within seventy-five yards of the *Happy Landings*. The ketch was all lighted up like Christmas and it sounded like a party was going on inside. Its captain and crew were doing a little celebrating, having completed the tough part of their mission and, no doubt, having earned a big fat payday.

As Bolan and Virgilio approached the estuary entrance, the smell of wood smoke drifted past. There were lights on in some of the birding shacks set in the hillside. Nobody was outside or on the beach. Night wasn't a good time to go exploring, unless you had a death wish.

The starlight reflected off the surf breaking over the bar. The tide was still coming in. Bolan figured he had an hour at the encampment, tops, to complete his business, before the tide started to turn. He had to time his exit just right so as to get over the sandbar, or he'd be stuck on the Osa for a complete six-hour tide cycle.

Virgilio steered them close to the shoreline, but not too close. The estuary narrowed a short distance farther, and the seaway split into a series of mangrove-lined channels, creating a veritable maze. Without hesitation, working in the half-light of stars, the *indio* selected one of the lanes and steered them up it.

Bolan noticed that the sound of the jet boats had stopped. They had reached their destination somewhere ahead in the darkness.

Coming across an enemy in this section of river would be tough, he thought. The quarters were tight. The dugout canoe could turn, but only just barely. Even in broad daylight, there was no way to see what lay around the next turn.

In the space of the next hundred yards, the river's many channels came together and became one.

After another hundred yards, Virgilio turned the bow toward a muddy bank near a towering tree draped with parasitical vines. The bow slid up on the bank and Bolan hopped out. He tied the canoe off on a log.

In the starlight, he could see a wall of reedlike plants with narrow, flat leaves. If anything, the insect noise was even louder there. It made his skin feel like it was vibrating.

There was no path that he could make out.

Virgilio handed him a roll of duct tape. They cut off strips and taped the cuffs of their BDU pants to their ankles to keep insects and other creatures from crawling up their legs.

As they shouldered the packs, Virgilio said, "Many coral snakes, maybe a crocodile. We go that way." He pointed up the side of the muddy bank.

Bolan pulled on his night-vision goggles. They turned the world lime-green and lemon-yellow. A yellow Virgilio was looking at him strangely. "I have another pair of night-vision goggles if you want to wear them," he told the *indio*.

"My eyes work fine," Virgilio said, unsheathing his machete. "We go now."

Bolan picked up the cased sniper rifle and followed him up the slippery bank and into the reeds.

Virgilio's advance was careful and efficient. His machete made a soft *swish* as he cleared trail. The soldier could see very little but his guide's back. In reality, there wasn't much else to see. The reeds were taller than his head and they were everywhere. The night-vision glasses allowed him to maintain a constant distance from Virgilio, and therefore keep from accidentally walking on his heels. If there were snakes or crocodiles, Bolan didn't see them. The bugs were hard to miss, though. And they bit him, despite the layers of repellant he had applied.

The only good thing about this leg of the trip, he thought, was that no human enemy could lie in wait along it to ambush them. The mosquitoes would have sucked him dry in a matter of minutes.

After a steady fifteen minutes of trekking, they came out of the flat swampy area and stopped at the foot of a forested hill. The jungle towered above them. Under the hundred-foot-high canopy, the darkness was absolute. No starlight penetrated the roof of branches, leaves and vines. An animal, a bird or a monkey, screamed from the depths.

Virgilio broke out the canteens and they drank.

The strap of Bolan's goggles was soaked with sweat, his hair matted, face and arms slick.

"We're still a long way from the camp," Virgilio said. "We have to climb this ridge and cross over to the other side. The river makes a big bend farther on. The traffickers are there."

The guide paused to drink more water, then he screwed the lid back on his canteen. "We'll follow a dry creek up to the ridge," he told Bolan as he took a Petzl headlamp from his pants pocket. "I have to use this light to find the way. You must be careful and try to step where I step. Snakes like the streambed. You won't be able to see them in the dark, even with your goggles. Don't touch anything here. Bad insects. Bad plants. It will make you sick quickly."

"No problem," the Executioner said. He took a pair of skintight, black leather combat gloves from his pocket and put them on.

Virgilio switched on his lamp and they began the climb. Because the low-intensity light was directed forward and above, Bolan had no trouble seeing where he was going. They scrambled up the rocky streambed. On both sides the big trees were fairly widely spaced. The forest floor was clean of undergrowth, barren even. Not enough sunlight penetrated the canopy to sustain grass or other low-growing plants.

Virgilio's headlamp swung back and forth as he scanned the creek bed before him. His machete, which had been still for many minutes, suddenly flicked out in a blur. The flat of the blade made a *smack* as it hit something solid. The something was four feet long, and the powerful blow flipped it through the air, sending it crashing into a heap of fallen leaves at the base of a balsa tree.

Virgilio stepped over to the stunned snake and brought the edge of the machete down once. As the headless thing thrashed in the leaves, Bolan tipped up his goggles. In the light of Virgilio's lamp, the snake's fat belly was white, its back was brown, black and white. The Executioner recognized the markings. *Fer-de-lance.* The camouflage was so good that laying belly down on the leaves, the viper became almost invisible.

The *indio* smiled at him and continued.

When he got within twenty feet of the ridge Virgilio stopped. "Careful as we go over up there," he said. "Keep low, otherwise the men in the valley might see us. They have goggles like yours, too." He looked at the terrain above, memorizing it, then shut off his headlamp.

Bolan followed the guide to the crest and, crossing it, looked over. Nestled in the narrow but deep valley below them, where the Rio Verde cut through a layer of harder rock, was the camp, lighted by banks of flood-lights. It wasn't a quiet place. He could hear the sounds of men and machinery, the steady hum of generators. Intervening tree trunks and branches obscured the details of the camp's layout.

"You can take off the pack, now," he told Virgilio, tipping his goggles up on top of his head. "This is as far as you go."

"I'll come with you," the first mate said, brandishing his machete.

"No, you don't."

"I'll wait for you, then," Virgilio said as he shrugged out of the pack straps.

The Executioner didn't need an escort any farther. He didn't know how he was coming out of the jungle. Or even if. "Go back to the canoe," he told his guide. "Get out of the river mouth before the tide turns. I can handle everything from here."

Bolan opened his pack and started pulling out gear and laying it on the ground. He took off his T-shirt and put on the armored vest. On top of that went the combat harness. He holstered the Beretta and slipped the sub-machine gun's lanyard over his head. The Steyr he shouldered by its strap. He did the same for his C-4 satchels. The preparation took no more than a couple of minutes.

"There are too many men down there, *Señor*," Virgilio protested a final time. "Too many guns, too many booby traps. You will never come out. You will die."

"Maybe. It's not your problem. Goodbye, friend."

The two shook hands, then Bolan switched on his goggles and started walking away, along the spine of the ridge. He followed it toward the river, hoping to get a more complete view from an overlook, a spot where the canyon's span broke the flow of the vegetation. He soon found a rocky outcrop below the canopy and edged out onto it. He wasn't too concerned about the possibility of being infrared scanned by the hostiles below. The residual daytime heat coming off the cliff would hide him well enough for the few seconds that he'd be exposed. He immediately pushed his night-vision glasses back on top of his head. He didn't need them.

From his new vantage point below the roof of the rain forest, Bolan saw what the satellite couldn't. He saw the Rio Verde's reverse S-curve, brightly illuminated by floodlights attached to tree trunks and set up on stanchions. The fleet of jet boats were tied gunwale to gunwale along a short strip of beach. Farther upstream was a makeshift wooden footbridge, spanning about seventy feet of river.

All of the compound's buildings were on the far side of the river from Bolan. There was a long, tent-style barracks and a smaller structure that looked like a cookshack. The helicopter pad was set in an area cleared of trees. Near the helipad, fifty-five gallon drums, probably fuel, were lined up. Another group of drums stood closer to the river and the jet boats.

While the Executioner watched, men in camouflage uniforms off-loaded cargo from the jet boats. They carried it by hand, up the bank, to a prefab building a short distance away. The entire camp, with the exception of the area near the boats, was strung with coils of concertina wire.

Bolan drew back from the edge, committing the details to memory. Then he took a second look. A bunker system, made of logs stacked and heaped with dirt, controlled the bend in the river. Alternating hardsites on either bank, above and below the footbridge, commanded both water and land access. Other bunkers, built deeper in the forest, surrounded the main complex, dominating the approaches with concentrated fields of fire.

He counted six bunkers. He estimated that there had to be three or four more in the trees, guarding the south and east sides of the compound.

The Executioner stepped back and checked his watch. It had taken him a little longer than he'd figured to get this close. From his bird's-eye recon of the camp, he could only see one way in, and he was a long way from the entry point. He still had enough time to do the job before the tide turned, but only if he picked up the pace. Which meant lightening his load. He immediately started shedding battle gear.

Bolan leaned the Steyr SSG P-IV against the base of a tree. Beside it, he dropped the SMG, its extra magazines and one of the high explosive satchels. Down to his combat harness, his Beretta and one satchel charge, he pulled the goggles over his eyes and backtracked his route along the ridge. Then he started his descent, hustling through a yellow-green landscape of infrared.

If there were booby traps waiting, he figured that they would be set fairly close to the earthen bunkers. Otherwise, it would take too many mines to cover the area. Concentrating the antipersonnel ordnance near the complex would bring any attackers under fire from the bunkers as well. In theory, at least, it made sense.

Heading down, even with the lighter load, was a tough hike because of the heat and humidity. Bolan followed a game trail that wound around the massive tree trunks. The sawing, droning bugs covered the sound of his running footfalls.

Ten minutes later, he reached the river. He had circled above the encampment. Along the bank was a well-traveled trail, the vegetation crushed under his boots. Bolan watched a log float past. The river was running quickly. Flipping up his night-vision goggles, he stepped across the trail, into the muck of the shoreline. He waded out a few feet and splashed some water on his face. It felt cool.

Around the bend downriver, the forest canopy was underlit by a soft, yellow glow. The hum of the camp's generators competed with the buzz of insects.

When the Executioner heard footsteps coming toward him, he reacted at once, backing out of the water and into the trees along the shore. He was taken a bit by surprise. He hadn't figured a night patrol would range so far from the compound. As he backed up, he saw the deep tracks he'd left in the soft mud of the riverbank.

He drew the Beretta from shoulder leather and tested the airtight seal of the sound-suppressor tube against the muzzle crown.

The men came closer, breaking twigs, talking softly. Maybe they were tired. Maybe they were in a hurry to get back to camp. Maybe they were careless enough to miss the tracks he'd left.

From behind a screen of strangler vines, Bolan watched four men appear along the near side of the bank. They were all in camouflage BDUs, all carrying M-16s and wearing night-vision goggles.

The man in the lead suddenly stopped the file with a raised hand. He pointed down at the mud.

The Executioner opened fire from ambush. The Beretta 93-R spit a series of subsonic rounds. There was just enough blow-back from each discharge to cycle the action. The low recoil allowed Bolan to shoot quickly, with minimum recovery due to muzzle climb. He moved from target to target, working from left to right, squeezing off head shot after head shot. He couldn't risk the possibility that they were wearing body armor. They had to go down and stay down. The leader took the last shot. From the expression on his face, he knew what was coming and he knew he couldn't do anything about it. In the instant before he was struck, he heard the sound of slugs slapping flesh, cratering bone. The men behind him collapsed like dominoes. Then the muzzle pointed at him from behind the tree flashed yellow-white and his skull exploded. The leader fell into the edge of the river with a loud splash.

Bolan stepped out of cover and grabbed the man by the ankle before the current drew his body downstream. He pulled the body up on the shore. The patrol leader had a walkie-talkie clipped to his web belt. If there was an upcoming scheduled communication check with the camp, this guy was going to miss it, which would set off alarm bells. The mission's numbers were falling in a blur, now. Without the element of surprise, the Executioner had no chance of success or of survival.

He pulled a strip of the duct tape off his ankle and stuck it over the Beretta's muzzle to keep out any mud and as much water as possible. He also put a strip over the pistol's ejection and magazine ports for the same reason. He slipped the Beretta back in its holster and looped the tab over the hammer spur. A quick check of his combat harness told him that everything else was battened down.

Instead of waiting for the river to provide another suitably large log, Bolan searched the near bank for something that would work. Upriver, he found a four-foot chunk of tree in the shallows. One end of it looked like it had been chainsawed, the other had a big clump of branches, with the leaves still on it. The log's diameter was about two feet. He used the stub of a broken branch to pull it free of the mud, then slid it deeper into the water. The thing barely floated.

It would have to do.

The Executioner put his night-vision goggles in a harness pouch, then he slung the satchel on top of the log and secured the strap to the branches. Though the canvas bag was khaki, it didn't blend in very well. Bolan couldn't risk someone noticing it. He scooped up double handfuls of mud and covered the package of explosives with it.

That done, Bolan pushed the log ahead of him, out into the main flow of the river. Here, the stream was forty-five feet across. It widened somewhat around the curve that fronted the camp.

When he got out waist deep, the water was colder. The current sucked his legs downstream. As he moved out farther, he lowered himself deeper and deeper into the water. He could see the lights around the bend below him. He could also see one end of the footbridge. And if anyone was looking his way, they could see him, too.

Submerged to his chin, his butt bouncing on the bottom, Bolan gripped the branched end of the log. When he lifted his heels from the streambed, he began to drift with the log down toward the light and the noise of the camp. He had to expose himself for a moment or two to get his drift lined up. To do this, he sighted down the side of the log.

On the left-hand bank, some hundred yards away, he could see men moving in the camp. If things didn't work out, he'd be facing a gauntlet of bunkers and a full-auto killzone. If he was seen, the drug soldiers would have a field day shooting at him, taking turns as he drifted past. On the bright side, he was just one guy going in. A guy without ID, without connections to the U.S. government. If he died this night, there'd be no back-splatter.

The current picked up noticeably as the water grew even shallower. The Executioner kept his back to the bottom. He didn't want some obstruction catching on the safety pins of the grenades strapped to his chest. He drew his head into the nest of branches and leaves and lowered his chin into the water, until just his nose and mouth stuck out. He hoped that no one would bother to look closely enough to see that he wasn't part of the tree.

Sucking in a deep breath, he lifted his knees higher and let the river sweep him down to meet whatever fate had in store.

OUT OF SIGHT, Virgilio watched the tall man unsling the beautiful rifle and set it against the tree. He watched as the American dropped the submachine gun and other things, and then without a backward glance, hurried away from this treasure trove, heading down the slope toward the river.

This greatly puzzled Virgilio. Why had they bothered to carry all that stuff up there if he wasn't going to use it?

The *indio* waited for a moment, out of politeness, then crossed the rocky outcrop to the abandoned gear. He couldn't believe his luck. He picked up the SMG first, hefting its weight in his hand. It was a serious weapon. He had seen guns like it in videos that Vorhees had showed him. He knew what it could do. *Rambo* was one of his all-time favorite movies.

Putting down the H&K, Virgilio picked up the rifle. At once, he was in love. The weapon had perfect balance. It was short and quick to point. The ideal rain forest gun. He cycled the bolt twice, ejecting the first cartridge from the magazine. Well, maybe not ideal, he thought, as he turned the round over in his fingers. A bullet that big would turn a white-faced monkey into a pile of bloody rags.

It was a big-game cartridge. Suitable for wild boar, crocodile, jaguar. All of which were in relatively short supply, even in the protected reserve of the national park.

After a few moments, he figured out how to get the lens covers off the night-vision telescope. It took him a bit more fiddling to find the on switch. Pulling the Steyr's stock to his cheek, he looked through the night sight, and was amazed at what he saw.

True enough, things were strangely discolored, but he could make out incredible detail in the darkest areas of the canopy.

He moved to the edge of the outcrop, dropped to his belly and took aim at the camp below. It had grown since he'd last seen it. More buildings and many more soldiers to protect the drugs. With his finger outside the trigger guard, Virgilio placed the center post on one man, then another. They seemed close enough to reach out and touch.

His trigger finger itched. He rubbed it on the rock to ease the tickling sensation.

What to do? he asked himself as he lowered the rifle. The situation was most confusing. Should he take his wonderful booty and make a run for the canoe? Or should he stay here and use the weapons the way they were meant to be used?

If he took the stuff out of the park, he knew he'd have to hide it. He'd never be able to show it to anyone for fear they'd blab the news all over, which would inevitably result in someone hitting him over the head or stabbing him in order to steal it. The other possibility was that he could sell it. Probably for quite a good price. The trouble was, cash was of little value to him. Where he lived, how he lived, there was nothing to spend it on.

If he left the tall man to fight this battle alone, he was convinced more than ever that the job was doomed to end badly. He had just seen how shockingly lopsided the odds were. A few well-placed bullets from on high might change the course of the fight. Just like in the movies.

Go or stay?

Stay or go?

In the end, Virgilio had only one choice.

15

Rio Verde camp, 12:15 a.m.

Roberto Murillo dry swallowed two more of Dr. Perpuly's pain pills. The bottle was already two-thirds empty. The medication seemed no longer to have much of an effect. The sutured half of his face throbbed horribly. With each pulsation the skin seemed to stretch to the splitting point. The infection had spread. He was certain of it. His body was racked with chills, then it was on fire. His thoughts were erratic, irrational and racing at light speed.

El Azote was a man who above all needed to be in control.

Now he was anything but.

One eye covered by bandages, his leg practically useless, infection raging throughout his system, he found himself in the clutches of the Colombian narcoterrorist, Enrique Tomás. Instead of being taken to meet with Samosa, as had been promised, Murillo had been hurried off to this tropical hellhole.

A hostage.

Soon, perhaps, to be a victim.

He sat on the edge of a bunk in the main barracks of the drug lord's rain forest camp. There were no screens on any of the windows, no glass in them, either. The floodlights from the work outside drew more bugs than he would have ever thought possible.

Roberto Murillo stared at the mosquito netting draped over the bunk. How many clung to the far side of the netting, sticking their pointed sucker stabbers through the mesh, hoping for a chance to bite him? A hundred thousand? Two hundred thousand? The air throbbed with the shrill whine of their beating wings. Maybe they smelled his infected wounds. Maybe the smell drove them wild.

For an instant, he felt a panic more powerful than anything he had ever experienced. He had a sense of being slowly, but inexorably, smothered by this jungle, by the sheer oppressive weight of its ravenous life. If Ramon didn't succeed in rescuing Samosa's children, he knew he would die there and the bugs would feast on his carcass.

In the Baja, Murillo would have stood a fighting chance. He would have had his own army to back him. Here, no one would come to his aid. He was the only Mexican in the camp. The rest were either Colombian Shining Path or ex-Noriega Panamanian paramilitaries, all men who'd been involved with the Samosa cartel unofficially for years. They knew where their daily bread came from, and what their lives depended on. To the soldiers outside, he was just another lump of meat.

Easy to kill.

There was no guard placed on him. There was no need of one. Even if he'd had the strength, there was nowhere for him to run. He had been under house arrest in the barracks since he'd arrived by helicopter with Tomás and his crew.

Roberto was being held hostage to insure the return of his half brother. He knew that Ramon wouldn't let him down. He trusted Ramon more than anyone. If there was a way to get him out of this mess, Ramon would find it.

Another, darker thought occurred to him. If things went badly, if he was killed, he knew that his brother would take revenge. Terrible revenge.

The tarp over the door at the end of the barracks pushed back and Tomás entered with another man, the camp commander. He was a Panamanian, a former officer in Noriega's private guard. Tomás shook the netting over Murillo's bunk, making the mosquitoes fly off. The bugs didn't seem to bother the Colombian. He didn't sweep them aside. He didn't have to. They didn't land on his skin.

Too nasty even for mosquitoes to bite, Murillo thought.

"I just had word from Don Jorge," Tomas said. "About your brother."

"And...?" Murillo said, impatiently.

"The news is very disappointing."

Murillo's heart stopped. Sweat poured down the sides of his face.

"I won't have the pleasure of staking you out on a fire ant mound and listening to your shrill, womanly screams," the Colombian said. "At least not this night. The Ortiz children are in the hands of the Don. From all accounts, your brother did a good job at the safehouse where they were being held. All but one of the Feds were killed in the operation. He brought the live one back with him as a captive. A very high-ranking Fed, as it turns out. Quite a catch, for a Mexican. Apparently, this American has information about the unfortunate incidents of the past few days, starting with the Yucatán, where your brother left my compadres to be slaughtered like pigs.''

"My brother didn't desert your men," Murillo protested. "They were attacked after he had left the scene."

"Convenient. But the end result is remarkably similar to what happened at the Hotel Flores, don't you think? Everybody shot to hell, while Ramon Murillo escapes without a scratch. I find that suspicious."

"I didn't escape without a scratch."

Tomás grinned. "Yeah, you got caught pretty good," he said. "But that changes nothing. My compadres are still dead. The Don is still out a hotel and a depository full of gold."

"My brother and I had nothing to do with any of that. This federal agent that Ramon captured, he will straighten everything out. The Murillos have been targeted by the U.S. government. Everything that's been done has been aimed at ruining our reputation."

"If this Fed doesn't give up what he knows," Tomás said, "or if he denies this conspiracy of yours, you will scream for me, yet, *Mexicano*. There's a debt of blood to be paid for the men we lost in the Yucatán. A debt of blood and pain."

Despite the threat, Murillo's spirits soared. The Colombian couldn't hold him against his will any longer. Under Ramon's careful torture, the American prisoner would tell the truth about everything, and explain to Samosa's satisfaction the string of disasters that had befallen them. Things would return to normal. The Murillos would regain their position of trust and honor in the cartel.

"Has the interrogation of the federal agent started, yet?"

"How the hell should I know?"

"I have to be there when it does."

Tomás scowled and spit on the floor, hugely unimpressed by the display of self-righteous fury.

"When can I leave here to meet my brother?"

"You can go right now, if you like," Tomás told him. "No one will stop you if you want to walk or swim."

"What about the helicopter?"

"It won't be back here until daylight. Relax and enjoy yourself. You've got six more hours in paradise."

16

The current drew Bolan and his log closer to the left bank, into the intense glare of the floodlights. As he drifted along, he could see into the firing slit of the first bunker on that side. He saw the muzzle and flash hider of the M-60 machine gun that was mounted there. Over the river and compound, swarms of insects billowed in the hard light. Along the riverbank, men in fatigues worked with bandannas over their mouths to keep from inhaling them by the thousands and choking on the dry, crisp wings.

If the drug soldiers in the bunker had seen him clinging to the log, it would have been over in the blink of an eye. Point-blank with the machine gun. Instant stew meat.

But they didn't notice. They were busy.

Logs drifted by all the time.

None of the camp guards expected trouble to sweep down on them from upriver, from the most remote, tangled heart of the rain forest preserve. With the sentry patrols, if there was trouble coming, they expected early warning of it.

Ahead, around the side of the log, he could see the footbridge coming up fast. Men were crossing it.

Men with automatic rifles.

The Executioner didn't dare dig his heels into the

streambed and slow the log. He didn't want anything to appear out of the ordinary to call attention to the drifting wood. An unnatural hesitation could mean discovery.

The men crossing the bridge paid the chunk of wood no mind as it swept below them. They were hurrying to get their work done, to get the new shipment of drugs packed away, and get out of the bug swarms.

Bolan saw the soles of their boots through the bridge's decking as he passed silently underneath.

He glided past two more bunkers without raising an alarm. Kicking his legs, he angled the log even tighter to shore on the left. The jet boats had been half dragged up onto the beach on that side and were tethered there. As the log drifted close to the sterns, the Executioner reached around for the strap on the satchel. Gripping it, he released his hold on the log and, as he fell away from it, pulled under by the weight of his loaded combat harness, the canvas bag came with him. Underwater, he rolled to his stomach and pulled himself along the stream bottom to the shallows.

When he reached the boats, he surfaced between a pair of hulls and sucked in a lungful of air. The jet boats' sterns had been pulled downriver by the current. The staggered boat hulls blocked him from the view of the bunker directly across the stream.

Dragging himself forward, Bolan crawled onto the shore, dripping, half out of the water. Resting on an elbow, he unholstered the 93-R and stripped off the duct tape. He drew back the slide to check for water down the muzzle and found the action dry. He took the sound suppressor from his harness, blew down its bore, then screwed it tightly to the barrel.

All the while, over the sawing of the insects and the hum of the power generators, he could hear men talking.

On the other side of the low, undercut bank, up a short trail, was the big prefab building he'd seen from the ridge. The storage shed. He visualized it in detail from memory. A single floodlight hung from the top of its eaves, casting a pool of light between its entrance and the river's edge. He counted the voices as best he could and came up with four talkers. At least four. The drug soldiers were standing in front of the entrance to the shed. Maybe taking a break from the off-loading.

Bolan needed to be up and moving before they saw him. He crawled farther out of the water and aimed the 93-R at the floodlight near the roof of the shed.

Lost in the din of bugs and generator, the Beretta coughed once, spitting a smoking hull onto the beach. With a faint tinkle of broken glass, the light winked out.

The men by the shed doorway looked up, then cringed as glass shards showered them. They weren't suddenly surrounded by pitch-dark. The other floods were still lighted. But the path from the beach to the shed was much dimmer. The breaking drug soldiers had leaned their automatic weapons against the wall of the shed. Sensing danger, one of the men grabbed a weapon. He didn't have time to shoulder it.

The Executioner was already running at them. As he charged up the bank and onto the path, the Beretta chugged in his fist. The first shot hit one of the men in the throat, sending him stumbling back through the open, hangar-type doorway. Bolan walked fire up the guy's face—chin, nose, forehead. A puff of pink brains haloed his head as his knees buckled and he dropped. The sight of the big man bearing down on them, gun blazing, froze two of the remaining three soldiers.

The third guy was the one with the M-16 in his hand. Bolan shot him in the center of his chest from fifteen away. He shot him twice, slamming him back into the shed's aluminum wall. The rifle slipped out of the gunner's grip as he slid down the dented wall. Meanwhile, the two frozen hardmen came unstuck from their fear. They both turned tail, running as fast as they could for the corner of the building.

The Executioner shot them both, one round each, in the back of the neck as he jumped the corpse in the doorway and rushed into the shed.

As he did so, there were shouts of alarm from behind.

He didn't expect to get far without drawing some attention, either from the men in the central camp or from the machine gun bunker opposite. It was pretty obvious he wasn't one of the cartel's crew. He was taller than anyone else, dripping wet and killing men.

The ceiling of the shed was twenty-five feet above him. Bare lightbulbs were strung on the metal rafters. The floor was made of pounded dirt, the air seething with flying bugs. The drugs were off the ground, stacked on wooden pallets. The shed easily held twenty times the coke he'd seen stuffed down the sailboat's bilge. The place was packed with it. The piles of cocaine bricks stood chest high, covering all but a few narrow aisle spaces. A center aisle ran down the middle of the shed to the rear hangar doors.

The men inside had been busy moving product, double counting the new stuff as it was piled on the pallets. To do this, some of them were standing on top of the heaps.

At the sight of one of their own, staggered by gunshots, blown back into the shed, the workers dropped their clipboards. By the time Bolan closed the gap to the doorway, they were already lunging for their weapons.

Automatic fire ripped the air as Bolan penetrated the

shed. A gunner balanced on a pile of cocaine shot from the hip at a rapidly moving target. Bullets sailed past the Executioner, whipping a flurry of holes in the heaped packages behind him.

Bolan fired back once, and the man spun to a knee, blood gushing from his neck. The soldier tried to bring his weapon up, and Executioner shot him again, this time in the temple.

The rest of the troops were yelling at him, at each other, jumping on the pallets of dope, trying to get an angle so they could fire without hitting members of their own team.

But the Executioner had a plan. The guys working in the storage shed weren't part of the picture, unless they got in his way. He pulled the ripcord on the satchel charge and underhanded it down an aisle between the heaps of drugs. The armed explosive hit the side wall and slid to the ground.

He didn't break stride. He was running for the door at the far end of the building.

A remote detonator rode on one of the chest straps of his combat harness. If, by any chance, he didn't live long enough to trigger the explosive, it would detonate without his help in five minutes.

Three drug soldiers blocked his exit.

From their expressions, he could see they didn't have a clue what was happening, or why. Some big bastard was streaking through the storehouse. A big bastard coming right at them.

As they raised their weapons, Bolan shot them. Fingers convulsed on triggers as the soldiers fell back, discharging wild gunfire in all directions. Amid the clattering din, Mack Bolan crashed past them, dashing through the back door of the shed.

Outside, the chaos was starting to build. Men all over the camp were yelling and running. To his left was the helicopter pad and the fuel storage area. Farther on, he could see the backside of a bunker. Someone opened fire from the bunker doorway. Bullets stitched along the ground, kicking up puffs of dirt as he sprinted for cover behind the dozen or so fifty-five-gallon drums lined up near the landing pad.

There was a shout and the shooting stopped at once. Someone had realized that hitting one of the drums was a very bad idea. There were roughly five hundred gallons of aviation fuel sitting in the middle of the camp.

Crouched behind the drums, Bolan unsheathed his SEAL-2000 knife. One of the drum lids had a pump handle attached to it. With a single swipe of the heavy blade, he cut through the handle's hose. Then he dumped the half-full drum onto its side, allowing the high-test fuel to spill out onto the dirt around the bases of the other drums.

When Bolan took off running again, moving from the fuel depot across open ground, many guns fired at him. The slugs came every which way, slamming into the tree trunks, skimming off the dirt. As he reached the plywood wall of the cookshack it turned to splinters.

The opposition was getting its act together.

As Bolan no longer needed the sound suppressor, he quickly dumped it and the matching subsonic ammo magazine. The new mag he slapped into place was loaded with full-power metal-jacketed 9 mm rounds.

Beyond the cookshack were the camp generators. There were three lined up under a wooden roof, mounted on a concrete pad.

As he reached to his harness for a fragmentation grenade, there was a rush of movement in the glassless, screenless window opening directly above him. A guy, probably the cook, had shoved an M-16 out the window and was frantically trying to line up a kill-shot.

If the gunner had taken his time, if he hadn't been holding his breath, he might have done it. But the cook was in too much of a panic. He cut loose with a howling burst of unaimed bullets, lighting up the night.

Bolan brought up the 93-R in a blur, firing through the flimsy wall a foot below the bottom of the window, where he figured the guy's chest had to be. A triangle of 9 mm holes bored through the unpainted plywood. With a moan, the cook dropped the rifle out the window and, as he did so, his head and shoulders slipped out of sight. There was a loud thud and a crash of pots inside the shack.

Bolan yanked the pin on the grenade and, letting the safety lever flip off, he underhanded the frag at the generators. The grenade bounced once in the dirt, hopping onto the concrete pad. Drawing back behind the cover of the building, the Executioner dug into his harness pouch for the night-vision goggles.

WHEN THE FIRST BURST of autofire cut loose, Roberto Murillo practically jumped out of his skin. The flinch was instinctive, part of the post-traumatic stress syndrome from the Baja disaster. As his heart thudded in his throat, Murillo told himself that it couldn't be happening again. One of the jerk-off Panamanians had to be shooting at a monkey or something.

As gunfire rattled from all over the camp, as men began to scream and shout, it became all too apparent that this wasn't the case.

They were under attack.

Just when Murillo thought he was home free, it was

all coming apart again. Everywhere he went, catastrophe seemed to follow. Men died, treasure was lost.

He had a chilling thought.

Was the same enemy still tracking him? Had the man with pale blue eyes followed him all the way to this rain forest hellpit? The one who wouldn't die, or couldn't be killed?

Murillo had no intention of waiting around to find out. He threw off the mosquito netting and slipped off the bunk, hobbling as fast as he could for the barracks' exit. He had to drag his wounded leg behind him.

Outside, the firefight was rapidly growing in intensity. Stray bullets sailed overhead as he sneaked a peek out the doorway. At that moment, Murillo tasted the same mindless chaos that had engulfed his Baja rancho. There were even more men here. More than at the San José depository, too. And they were well dug in. In his heart, he knew that despite all the preparations, no one in the camp was really ready for what was coming. What was coming was worse than anything any of them could ever imagine.

There was only one sure way out of this place, and he was going to take it. Murillo beat back the swarming insects. With his hand clamped over his mouth to keep from inhaling them, he limped across the compound toward the beached jet boats.

The drug soldiers ignored him as he hobbled past. They had other things to worry about. Murillo could feel the stitches in his leg breaking loose. By the time he reached the boats, his shoe was full of blood. Inside his sock his toes squished.

He caught hold of a mooring line and followed it down the embankment to the bow of one of the boats.

As he started to climb in, there was a tremendous bang and a big yellow flash from behind the cookshack.

Then all the camp lights went out.

WITH HIS GLASSES in place, the Executioner stepped out from cover. It was dark. Darker than dark. Blacker than black. No light penetrated the rain forest canopy. As if they'd been struck blind, the drug soldiers of the Samosa cartel stood in the open or crouched behind cover, still. Not even daring to breathe. To Bolan, they looked like yellow statues on a field of lime-green. As he walked among them, some of the men fumbled clumsily for their own night-vision optics.

He could have killed many, but he didn't.

He didn't have the time.

When the drug soldiers recovered, as they soon would, when they got their night-vision goggles on or found flashlights, they would immediately move to cut off his escape. And if he was still there, they would succeed.

Breaking into a trot, the Executioner made for the row of fuel drums on the bank above the jet boats.

Heavy machine gun fire clattered from the bunker across the river. A line of 7.62 mm NATO slugs ripped through the front of the big storage shed over his left shoulder.

The machine gunner had his night-vision optics on. And he had acquired his target.

Bolan pulled a Thunderflash grenade from his vest, primed it, then chucked it overhand in a high arc across the stream.

A frag might have done more permanent damage to the bunker, but only if Bolan could have thrown it through the foot-high machine gun slit. A virtually impossible feat under the circumstances. The stun grenade didn't need precision delivery.

The Executioner turned his face away from the river, covering his lenses with both palms.

Behind him, the Thunderflash detonated with an ear-splitting *whump*. Its airburst of intense light, multiplied thousands of times by the gunner's night optics, left him totally blinded.

It gave Bolan time to ram the point of his knife into the base of a fuel drum. Gasoline gushed in a cool stream over his fingers as he jerked the blade free.

In three more strides, he was on the beach. He slashed the mooring line to one of the jet boats and pushed it out into the current, stern first. As he swung a leg over the bow, a figure appeared from behind the side console. A man with a half-bandaged face rose from where he had been cowering on the deck.

The Executioner recognized him at once.

"Who is it?" Roberto Murillo pleaded into the darkness. "Who's there?"

Autofire hissed into the water, slugs thunking into the side of the welded aluminum hull.

Bolan shoved the man into the boat and hit the outboard engine's starter switch.

VIRGILIO LAY on his belly on the ridge, surveying the scene downrange through the Litton nightscope, waiting for the right moment to use his rifle. He'd watched the tall man enter the storage shed, but because of the angle of view, he couldn't see him when he came out the other side.

There was no way to miss the gunfire the gringo had drawn. The sound of one-sided battle rattled and echoed up the canyon.

Virgilio held his own fire because he didn't want to accidentally hit the man he was trying to help.

When the generators blew, and the world outside the Litton scope went instantly black, he was startled, but only for a moment. Snuggling back into the scope's eye-piece, he searched the camp. It was easy to pick out the tall man. He was the only one moving. Virgilio watched the American cross the center of the compound on a dead run toward the beach and the jet boats. Then a machine gun from a bunker on Virgilio's side of the river cut loose.

The *indio* had no shot.

The wrong side of the bunker faced him.

He swung his sights back on the tall guy, just in time to see him drop into a crouch. If Virgilio knew where the American was headed, and why, so did the machine gunner.

Virgilio didn't actually see the Thunderflash grenade sail across the river, but he couldn't miss the effect when it went off. The burst of light speared through the night-scope and into his right eye. Howling with pain, he let the weapon's butt slip from his shoulder.

ENRIQUE TOMÁS was on the far side of the compound, away from the river, when the shooting started. He and the Panamanian camp commander were doing a walking tour of the perimeter. At the sounds of gunfire, they stopped walking and started running, their side arms drawn, toward the source of the noise.

Before Tomás could advance more than halfway across the compound, the generators blew, and the lights went out. He was left standing in the open, totally vulnerable.

The shooting stopped.

The yelling stopped.

Tomás held his breath. Someone was running toward him. The Colombian couldn't move. He didn't know which way to go. Then he felt the rush of air, cool against his sweaty face as whoever it was hurried past, not three feet away.

After a second or two, a machine gun stuttered from the opposite riverbank. Tomás immediately dropped to a knee and instinctively turned his head aside as heavy slugs ripped through the pitch-black camp.

When the Thunderflash detonated over the river, his face was still turned away. Because his back was to the big show, he missed seeing the blinding white fireball. For a split second, the forest before him leapt into view, then it vanished again.

The machine gun went silent.

Almost at once, he heard more footfalls coming his way. Lots of them, this time.

He thought, this is it. Here it comes.

Instead of the bullet he expected in the back of the neck, someone pressed a pair of night-vision goggles into his hand. Tomás quickly pulled them on. He looked into the NOD-goggled, yellow-tinted face of the Panamanian captain. Six other soldiers were likewise equipped.

"He's trying to reach the boats," the Panamanian said.

With Tomás running tight on his heels, the captain sprinted for the riverbank. Halfway there, Tomás could see that one of the boats had been cut free. It was already in the river, drifting backward, away from the camp. The tall intruder was leaning over the side console. The jet boat's outboard cranked over, shattering the heavy stillness.

"Get him!" Tomás said, raising his pistol and firing.

As the other men aimed their assault rifles, a single gunshot boomed at them from downriver.

One of the soldiers sat hard and slowly rolled onto his side, drawing his knees up to his chest.

Sniper! Tomás thought. And even as he realized what was happening, the distant rifle boomed again.

A bullet whined a foot over his head.

This time, Tomás had seen the muzzle-flash high on the canyon ridge. So had the others.

As they shifted their aim, the jet boat's engine caught with a roar.

17

Virgilio wasn't aiming at the soldier he'd hit.

His intended target had been ten feet to the left and five feet lower. He might have jerked the trigger when he squeezed it. That could have explained the difference between aim point and bullet fall. And he certainly didn't have a clue as to how to read the distance scales on the scope's reticule. Despite never having fired this particular rifle before, and never having touched a night-scope in his life, he'd hit something, and that made him feel powerful. As if no matter what he did, he could do no wrong.

The gods of battle were on his side.

And on the side of the tall American he so much admired.

If he hadn't fired when he had, if he hadn't hit anything when he'd fired, the big man would have been a sitting duck in the boat in the middle of the river. The drug soldiers with their night-vision would have shot him to pieces.

In the heat of the moment, it didn't occur to Virgilio that if his opposition hadn't been so tightly clumped downrange, his bullet would have missed by a wide margin.

He cycled the Steyr's action and reacquired the sight picture, edging forward a bit on his belly on the outcrop to get more comfortable. This time, he held the center post midchest on a standing man. As he tightened his finger on the trigger, he relaxed and exhaled slowly. The trigger came back easily at first, then there was a hesitation, a noticeable increase in resistance. He added a touch more pressure, and the trigger broke. The short-barreled rifle roared and bucked against his shoulder.

He rode the recoil wave, bringing the scope back on target.

To his dismay, the man he'd aimed at was in the same spot, apparently untouched, although his stance had changed. He was now ducking his head. Everyone else in the group was still standing, too.

Before he could chamber a new round, all the riflemen along the river below him swung their weapons up.

They were pointing them right at him.

Virgilio cursed. As he started to push back from the edge of the ridge, gunfire chattered. Before he could retreat, a mad flurry of bullets bracketed his position. They ricocheted off the face of the outcrop in front of him, sparking, peppering his face and hands with hot chips of rock as the rounds slammed into the stone wall behind him.

In order to cover his eyes, he had to let go of the rifle.

He was too close to the edge. The Steyr not only dropped, it slipped forward over the curve of the weathered rock. He made a desperate grab for it. As he reached out, he was struck in the forearm by a .223 tumbler.

The shock made his arm go numb up to the shoulder.

Virgilio jerked back. As he pushed up from the rock and twisted away from the precipice, he was hit again, this time in the side. The impact knocked the wind out of him. A burning lance skewered his guts. The *indio* tried to throw himself away from the edge, but his legs suddenly had no strength. He literally went nowhere, but flopped flat on his belly, with bullets hailing around him and his boots kicking out into space.

Then he began to slide away, to slip over the curved edge of the outcrop. Clawing desperately with his one good hand, he couldn't get a sufficient grip to stop himself.

The gunshots from below ceased, their echoes rolled like thunder down the canyon.

Virgilio heard the jet boat's engine roar to life. The sound made him smile. He knew what it meant.

At least the tall man had a chance.

Then his tenuous grip on the boulder's curve gave way. The rock's surface brushed past him, and he fell backward into the darkness.

Screaming.

As THE RIVER pushed the jet boat away from the camp, Mack Bolan saw a half-dozen men charging across the compound toward him. Despite the camp's total blackout, they could see what they were doing. Like him, they were wearing night-vision glasses.

The soldiers raised their weapons and opened fire.

The river was pushing the boat away from danger, but not nearly fast enough.

As he pumped the throttle, a bullet shattered the console's Plexiglas windshield in front of him. Then, from behind and above his position, came the hard crack of a gunshot. He recognized the sound. The short-barreled Steyr made a hell of a racket.

On the riverbank, one of the soldiers went down hard. The others stopped shooting and started scanning the slopes for the sniper's hide.

Bolan cranked over the starter again. The Yamaha outboard howled to life. Without pause, he slammed the throttle down, gripping the wheel in both hands, using his main strength to bring the boat about, even as the 150-horse motor threw up a towering rooster tail of spray. The turn was tight, the distance to the opposite shore narrow, but he made it without running the boat aground.

From the beach, muzzles flashed as the drug soldiers swept the trees on the canyon rim opposite with gunfire.

Its engine running wide open, the jet boat hurtled into the humid darkness downriver. Over the high-pitched whine of the motor, the Executioner heard a scream.

A long, terrible scream.

He knew what it meant.

And he shut the meaning out of his mind.

With the wind buffeting his face, he fumbled over the jet boat's side console, flicking switches.

The bow searchlight blazed on. Directly ahead, the river turned starboard.

Bolan cut the wheel over, hard right. He had to, or he'd run the boat up a tree. The left side of the hull slammed into the river's undercut bank and bounced off. As it did so, Roberto Murillo was nearly thrown from the boat. He landed on a gunwale and bounced into the bilge compartment. Recovering, he clung to the middle thwart with both arms, kneeling on the deck as if in prayer. Looking up in the backwash of the bow's light and the red glow of the console's instrument panel, Murillo had his first glimpse of the man who was driving. From the expression of abject horror that passed over his face, it wasn't the happiest of revelations.

Meanwhile, at Bolan's end of the boat, everything was happening very quickly. The speed boat was traveling at better than fifty miles an hour. This section of river, which he'd never seen before, twisted and turned unpredictably. The Executioner had to concentrate to keep ahead of the game, to react in time to the surprises.

Preoccupied as he was, he still found the necessary half second to reach up to the strap of his combat harness and slap the face of the remote detonator.

Behind them, the world rocked.

On the other side of the ridge, a towering fireball erupted. It looked like half the forest was consumed by flame.

Seconds later, debris blown skyward started falling into the river all around them. Chunks of shattered wood and rocks hit the deck, but most of it landed in the water or in the trees beyond. Roberto Murillo covered his head with his hands.

"You killed them all!" he howled into the metal seat. "You killed them all!"

The Executioner surely hoped so.

"Who are you?" Murillo screamed.

Bolan didn't answer. He was too busy feathering the throttle, trying to cut the corners of the river's oxbows, maximizing speed without sending the jet boat flying off into the trees.

He came a bit too close to the left bank. A tree branch slashed through the boat. It caught Murillo across the back. It lifted him and sent him crashing hard against the front of the console.

"Oh, God," he groaned into his cupped hands. "Oh, God, my face."

"Stay down if you want to live," Bolan shouted at him.

The Executioner didn't see the log in front of them until it was too late to do anything about it. It was big, and they were traveling very fast. There was a sudden jolt, and the jet boat's bow leaped up. The rest of the boat followed, spearing into the air, outboard screaming. They slammed back down hard. Bolan fought to keep the boat on track as it skipped over the surface. Directly ahead of them, the river took another turn. They faced a rock wall that plummeted into the water.

Bolan jerked back on the throttle to kill their speed. It was either that or run head-on into the outcrop. As he did so, a flare of light swept over them from behind. A spotlight. And at the same instant, he heard the sounds of other engines, other boats, bearing down on them. Gunfire rattled from upriver, and a volley of bullets sang overhead, sparking off the rock face and sailing into the trees.

Pounding the throttle down with his fist, the Executioner raced around the turn, out of the line of fire.

ENRIQUE TOMÁS blazed away with his Glock from the shore, but he couldn't hit the tall guy at the jet boat's controls. The boat was moving too fast and it bounced wildly up and down as it climbed over its own wake.

In the boat, Tomás saw a second man. A man with a bandaged face, crouching. Fury gripped the Colombian as he realized what had happened. And that he could nothing to stop it.

Roberto Murillo, the betrayer, had made his escape.

This was all about the Mexican's escape.

Tomás ran after the Panamanian commander, who was already jumping into the waiting boats. The waves created by the fleeing jet boat created mild havoc on the shore, making the remaining vessels bang into each other. At the commander's shouted direction, his men cut the bowlines and backed the three boats into the water.

Tomás would have climbed into the lead boat, but the Panamanian started off before he could get a leg over the gunwale. The commander backed his around, and turning on his spotlight, roared off downriver in pursuit.

"Come on! Hurry!" Tomás said to the soldier driving the second jet boat as he climbed on board. "He's getting away!"

The driver gunned his engine, then with a sickening lurch of acceleration, raced after the Panamanian. When Tomás looked back, the third boat was still drifting away from shore. Its engine had flooded.

Tomás brought his eyes back to the front. It was white-knuckle time as the jet boat picked up even more speed. It felt like they were flying above the surface of the water rather than through it.

The Panamanian's boat disappeared around the first sharp turn ahead. As they reached the same spot, behind them, the camp exploded with a tremendous roar. Tomás turned to see an enormous ball of fire leaping into the night sky. The heat slammed him at the same instant as the shock wave. The shock wave that bowled over rain forest trees like matchsticks and turned the Rio Verde into a ribbon of mist.

Looking back into the inferno, Tomás glimpsed the third jet boat as it was completely swallowed up.

Everything was gone in an instant.

As the firelight peaked and started to fade, the stern of Tomás's jet boat was lifted by the surging wave. Stuff was crashing into the water and into the surrounding jungle. They made it around the river's bend just as shit really began to hit the fan. Flying tree limbs, chunks of rock, cartwheeling sections of the shed roof.

The driver poured on the speed to escape the worst of the falling debris. Behind them, in the dark, Tomás could hear the sounds of big trees still crashing over, trees weakened, then falling in delayed reaction to the explosion.

Ahead of them was the Panamanian's boat. They were gaining on it, steadily. As they rounded another tight turn, at the end of the straightaway before them, they could see the intruder's boat, pinned for an instant in the spotlight of the commander's jet boat. Then their quarry vanished around the next right.

"Faster!" Tomás yelled.

The lead boat's engine screamed as the Panamanian tried to close the gap with the enemy.

Tomás was watching when the commander's boat hit the hidden log and was airborne. Its spotlight played up into the trees as it soared through the air. Tomás could see the rock wall dead ahead. He knew there was no room for the Panamanian to stop. The boat was going too fast and it was out of control. It plowed headlong into the wall. First, he heard the sound of the crash, then a millisecond later, a billowing explosion as fuel tanks cracked and ignited. In the beam of his own spotlight, Tomás saw bodies flying through the air.

As the driver hauled back on the throttle to avoid a similar fate, they passed through what was left of the fireball that hung over the water. Tomás shielded his face with an arm to keep from being scorched.

The jet boat glided to a stop beside the blackened, impact-scarred rock face.

Caught in the spotlight, a dead man hung from the branches of a tree overhead. Half a dead man, to be exact. His blast-ripped torso trailed a ten-foot-long streamer of uncoiled guts.

"Go! Go!" Tomás shouted, pounding on the driver's shoulder with his fists.

FROM BEHIND HIM came the sound of a metal hull crashing into rock, then blowing apart. Bolan didn't look back. He didn't have to. The spotlight coming up on his stern had winked out. One of the pursuers was history.

The wind screamed through the bullet hole in the windshield in front of him. He had a fleeting glimpse of Virgilio's dugout, beached by the reeds.

Then it was gone. A passing blur.

It told him where he was and how far he had to go.

The spotlight picked out a long, straight track between low, grassy banks. Bolan glanced at his wristwatch. The tide was falling fast, now. It would continue to drop for another three hours. But in less than six minutes, by his calculations, the bar at the estuary mouth would be dry.

If he didn't beat the falling tide, he only had one option. He would have to turn and fight. He wasn't opposed to a final face-off and would have already made the play if it hadn't been for his passenger. He wanted to keep Roberto Murillo alive, if possible. The man had value. Trading value as well as informational value.

There was also the matter of him paying in full for his role in the death of Yovana Ortiz. Getting hit by a stray bullet was too merciful, too quick to be justice.

Then another spotlight played over the back of the boat. Almost immediately, gunfire chattered from behind and bullets zinged off the gunwales.

Bolan took evasive action, steering from side to side in the river channel, scraping sides of the hull against the mangrove roots. Slugs skimmed off the river's surface, whistling into the trees.

Before him, the mangroves opened onto the wider estuary.

The Executioner flattened the throttle.

ROBERTO MURILLO would have thrown himself overboard just to get away from the loco gringo, but the jet boat was going sixty miles an hour. The impact would have torn him apart, or knocked him unconscious. Either way, he wouldn't survive.

Hunkered in the bottom of the speeding boat with bullets raining all around, he knew that what he had felt earlier back at the camp, the sense of his own vulnerability, had been mere prelude. He had only thought he was out of control before.

In retrospect, the cruelties he'd suffered at the hands of Enrique Tomás and the other Colombians seemed inconsequential, even childish. Wherever this tall American went, disaster and destruction followed.

And the stone-faced bastard took it as a matter of course.

Murillo knew there were no survivors at the Rio Verde camp. The explosion was too huge, too unexpected. No one had time to run. And running wouldn't have done them any good. The steep canyon walls had contained and focused the force of the blast.

As for him, his own injuries, his face was ruined, he knew that. The whipping tree limb had ripped out all of the stitches. The numbness caused by the blow was starting to fade. With his fingertips he felt a great flap of flesh hanging loose under what was left of his bandage. Blood from the new damage soaked his shirtfront and made it stick to his skin.

It was the least of his worries.

As they raced across the flat, open water of the estuary, gunfire from the pursuing boat intensified. Perhaps they didn't know he was a captive of the gringo?

Or maybe they didn't care.

Murillo was unable to look into the wind rushing over the boat's bow. It cut under his bandage and lifted the torn flap of his face.

So he didn't see what lay ahead.

TOMÁS LET OUT a whoop of triumph when he saw the lines of white foam breaking across the estuary entrance. The tide had already run out. The intruder was trapped, as was the Mexican betrayer.

"He'll have to turn!" Tomás shouted into the driver's ear. "We've got him now!"

The driver nodded that he understood.

Then, to the two riflemen clinging to the bow, Tomás cried, "Nail him when he comes broadside! Shoot him to pieces!"

The riflemen nodded as well. They were ready.

As the distance to the Pacific rapidly shrank, instead of turning one way or another, the intruder drove straight at the waves breaking over the bar.

With a jolt, Tomás realized that the man wasn't going to stop.

BOLAN IGNORED the power-trim switch on the jet boat's throttle. With it, he could have tipped the jet drive up, making it run more shallow.

But speed was going to save the day.

Holding the outboard redlined at seven thousand, he aimed for the surf.

In front of them, he could see the bare sand, a line of it across the mouth of the lagoon. Every time a wave broke, then surged back, the shore was exposed. On the estuary side, there was a ledge, a sloping bank.

An exit ramp.

"Better hang on!" he shouted at Murillo.

The Mexican looked forward, saw what they were about to hit and buried his face in the bottom of the boat.

The impact was a thousand times worse than the river log.

The sandbar didn't give.

The jet boat gave.

The bottom of its hull concaved as it slammed into the bar. Then it flew, bow climbing, over the strip of wet sand. When it came down, it landed fifty feet away in the middle of the breakers. It also came down stern-first. One corner dug in, and the boat twisted sideways, plowing into an oncoming wave.

One second Bolan was behind the wheel, hanging on, the next he was hurtling through the windshield, then over the bow, before crashing headfirst into the warm sea.

He blacked out for a second. He breathed in salt water and choked, coming to at once. Popping to the surface, he realized he couldn't touch bottom. The outgoing tide had created a riptide that was pulling him out to sea. As he tread water, a light hit him. He turned and saw the other jet boat coming right at him. Right at the bar.

The drug soldiers were trying to do what he had done.

It was a bad idea.

They had the timing all wrong. Instead of skipping over the bar, they pancaked on it. The boat bounced high, inverting in midair and spilling its occupants into the surf.

"Help me!" someone cried in Spanish.

Bolan's jet boat had also overturned. It floated, hull up, thirty feet away. Roberto Murillo had survived the crash. He was clinging to the bow, waving his arm frantically. Bolan saw that the bow spotlight hadn't broken or shorted out, yet. It glowed eerily three feet underwater.

The Executioner started to make for the boat. He was ten feet away when he saw something swim past the submerged light.

Something big and black.

He brought himself up short, treading water.

Behind him in the surf, the drug soldiers started screaming. He could see them in the starlight. They were standing in waist-deep water, spinning around, splashing their arms.

They knew what he knew.

The sea was full of sharks.

From beside the overturned boat, Roberto Murillo let out a shrill yelp. It ended suddenly, in a heavy, gurgling splash.

When Bolan turned back, the Mexican was gone. Another long shadow passed in front of the submerged light. Then a boiling cloud of crimson.

The Executioner knew he couldn't stay there any longer. He started swimming with the current, away from the feeding frenzy in the near shallows.

The water was dark, the sky full of stars. He shut everything out, everything but the stroke and the kick. In his mind, he put an X through the Rio Verde storage camp.

18

Hal Brognola didn't know where he was.

Blindfolded, his hands cuffed behind his back, he sat in a hard wooden chair. His captors had relieved him of most of his clothes, leaving him in a T-shirt and boxer shorts. When he stamped his bare heel on the floor, the resulting echoes made the room sound empty. It was quite warm and the air was still.

Through the weave of the blindfold, he could see light. It got brighter at intervals when he turned his head. A series of big windows, he thought. No curtains on them. The walls might be white. He had a sense of being elevated, maybe on a second or third floor.

When he listened really hard, he could hear children's voices off in the distance, as if from a playground or a school.

There were no traffic sounds.

No cars. No planes. Nothing.

Which made him think he must be in a rural area.

Brognola slumped back against the chair. Part of him was hard-focused, totally professional, looking for an edge, something that would help him escape. Another part, equally pragmatic, saw that exercise as hopeless. He was playing games with himself to keep from going crazy, from confronting something that he wasn't ready to face.

Brognola didn't know why Ramon Murillo had kidnapped him along with the children. He didn't know why he was still alive.

After being grabbed at the hotel parking lot, he had been blindfolded and manacled. From the elapsed time between the kidnapping and their arrival at what had to be a small private airport, he knew they were still in the States. From the seating in that first plane, he figured it was a Cessna twin-engine. They had taken off and, after flying for several hours, had landed and immediately changed planes.

The aircraft switch was made once more before they reached their final destination. As he was rushed across the tarmac to a waiting limousine, the air felt hotter and much more humid, the sun more intense. The whole journey he had been surrounded by Spanish speakers. He still was.

He figured he'd been taken south.

How far south was the question.

On the other side of the room, a door opened. Hardsoled shoes crossed the floor toward him. Over the pounding of his own heart, the big Fed counted three or four men. He could smell their cologne and Havana cigars, and tequila on the breath of the man who roughly shoved him forward. Behind his back, the handcuffs were removed, and he was jerked to his feet and pulled from the chair.

No one said anything.

The silence in the room was heavy, expectant.

Then he heard tapping behind him. Someone was rapping lightly on the wall with a hammer. It made hollow sounds on the Sheetrock, then a solid thunk, as the hammerhead found a stud.

Two men gripped Brognola under the armpits and

lifted him. They slammed his back against the wall, holding him there. They let him slide down the wall a little, and he felt something under his feet. It felt like an orange crate or a wooden box.

"What are you doing?" he demanded, unable to contain himself any longer. "What do you want from me?"

More bodies leaned into him, squashing him against the wall. Brognola struggled but there were too many of them and they were too strong. They pushed so hard on his chest that he could barely breathe.

Two men grabbed his right arm and by force, straightened it out to his side and turned it palm forward.

Brognola still didn't have a clue. He was in denial.

When he felt a sharp point of pain in the center of his trapped hand, he realized what was about to happen to him, but it was already too late to do anything about it.

The hammerhead made solid contact with the nail. The nail point and shaft skewered Brognola's hand, pinning it to the wall, and sinking deeply into the stud behind.

A cry leaped from Brognola's throat.

It echoed in the empty room.

A second blow of the hammer buried the nail deeper.

The men released him and stepped back. They let the big Fed hang there for a moment, pondering his strange, new reality. Standing on trembling legs on the orange crate, his hand convulsed around the spike.

On the other side of the room, the door opened again. There were more footsteps, more men entered the room.

"There's someone here who wants to meet you," Ramon Murillo said to Brognola. "He wants to meet you face-to-face." With that, he ripped the blindfold from Brognola's eyes.

Shaking his head to clear it, Brognola looked into the

face of a man he had never seen before. Yet, he knew who it was, even before Murillo spoke again.

"Señor Fed," Murillo said, "may I introduce you to Don Jorge Luis Samosa, the Lord of the Seas."

*Don't miss the exciting conclusion of
the* LORD OF THE SEAS TRILOGY.
*Look for the Executioner #261, DAWNKILL,
on sale August 2000.*

STONY MAN® 48

Conflict Imperative

In order to end a long war with internal terrorist factions,
Peru agrees to hand over part of her sovereign territory
to a rebel coalition. The deal is brokered by a reformed
IRA terrorist, who is up for a Nobel prize for his
peacemaking efforts. But the man has his own agenda,
and Bolan is taken prisoner!

Available in August 2000 at your favorite retail outlet.

James Axler

OUTLANDERS®

HELL RISING

A fierce bid for power is raging throughout new empires of what was once the British Isles. The force of the apocalypse has released an ancient city, and within its vaults lies the power of total destruction. Kane must challenge the forces who would harness the weapon of the gods to wreak final destruction.